CELG

SO-ACA-920

JUN -- 2017

GOOD WATER

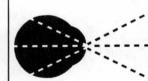

This Large Print Book carries the
Seal of Approval of N.A.V.H.

GOOD WATER

JOHN D. NESBITT

THORNDIKE PRESS

A part of Gale, Cengage Learning

GALE
CENGAGE Learning

Farmington Hills, Mich • San Francisco • New York • Waterville, Maine
Meriden, Conn • Mason, Ohio • Chicago

Copyright © 2016 by John D. Nesbitt.
Thorndike Press, a part of Gale, Cengage Learning.

ALL RIGHTS RESERVED
This novel is a work of fiction. Names, characters, places and incidents
are either the product of the author's imagination, or, if real, used
fictitiously.
The publisher bears no responsibility for the quality of information
provided through author or third-party Web sites and does not have
any control over, nor assume any responsibility for, information
contained in these sites. Providing these sites should not be construed
as an endorsement or approval by the publisher of these organizations
or of the positions they may take on various issues.
Thorndike Press® Large Print Western.
The text of this Large Print edition is unabridged.
Other aspects of the book may vary from the original edition.
Set in 16 pt. Plantin.

LIBRARY OF CONGRESS CATALOGING-IN-PUBLICATION DATA

Names: Nesbitt, John D., author.
Title: Good water / John D. Nesbitt.
Description: Large print edition. | Waterville, Maine : Thorndike Press Large Print,
   2017. | Series: Thorndike Press large print western
Identifiers: LCCN 2016055501| ISBN 9781410485823 (hardback) | ISBN 141048582X
   (hardcover)
Subjects: LCSH: Large type books. | BISAC: FICTION / Mystery & Detective /
   General. | GSAFD: Western stories.
Classification: LCC PS3564.E76 G66 2017 | DDC 813/.54—dc23
LC record available at https://lccn.loc.gov/2016055501

Published in 2017 by arrangement with Cherry Weiner Literary Agency

Printed in the United States of America
1 2 3 4 5 6 7 21 20 19 18 17

For Muñeco, in our hearts forever.

CHAPTER ONE

Tommy sat relaxed in the saddle as he scanned the landscape. The rangeland stretched away dry and faded in the heat of midsummer, with shimmering waves in a level area to the north. Nothing moved, not even a jackrabbit on the ground or a bird in the sky. Tommy gazed at the low hills to his left, where he expected Red to show up at any minute.

A thin hawk sailed into view above his hat brim. Tommy turned in the saddle and searched the country behind him. As far as he could see, no one was following or keeping an eye on him.

The horse shifted beneath him and made a low snuffling sound. Tommy settled back into his normal position and reached forward to pat the brown neck. The animal, warm and solid to the touch, let out a sigh.

The horse's head went up, and Tommy's eyes followed. Here came Red, raising a small trail of dust as the sorrel ranch horse moved at an easy lope. Tommy waited with his hands on the saddle horn. The horse's hooves drummed on the dry earth, and closer, the sound of the animal's breathing carried on the still air.

Red slowed the horse and brought him to a stop, with a jingling of bits and the rustle of leather. Red pushed back his hat, and his wavy red hair framed his face. His blue eyes settled on Tommy. "Hey, kid. Been waitin' long?"

"Just a few minutes." Tommy relaxed his shoulders, as if he had tensed them to toss off the word "kid" one more time. Red was only a couple of years older, and the men at the ranch called both of them kids, but when the two of them were off on their own like this, Red liked to set himself a notch above his pal.

The sorrel lowered its head to rub against a foreleg, and Red pulled the reins. Glancing at the sky and rubbing his forehead with the back of his hand, he said, "It's early yet. What do you say we take a little ride over east? I'd like to get a closer look at those girls."

"Do you think we should?"

"Don't you like girls?"

"Of course I do. But it's not part of our work."

"We've got our work done for the day. You checked your pasture, I checked mine, and we've got time to spare. Just enough to drop into Little Mexico, water our horses, and be good neighbors." Red lifted his chin and tipped his head back and forth. "Don't worry. Nobody's got to know about it except you and me."

"I don't think Vinch will like it."

"I just said, he doesn't need to know. To hell with him."

Tommy thought those were big words, even this far from the ranch headquarters. But he had seen the Mexican girls from a distance, too, when he and Red had ridden this way a few days earlier, and he hadn't forgotten. "Well, all right," he said. "But we'd better not stay long."

Red smiled with his clever expression. "Of course not."

They headed east with the horses at a fast walk. Red seemed to be making an effort to appear casual and confident. With his chin high, he was whistling "My Darling Clementine" and tipping his upper body back and forth with the shifting hooves of the ranch horse.

Tommy's eyes focused on an object up

9

ahead. "Looks like company," he said.

Red quit whistling and snugged his hat brim as he stared ahead. "Sure is." He adjusted his reins and settled into a serious posture.

Tommy said, "I wonder if he wants something."

Red lifted the corner of his mouth in a half-smile. "Everyone wants something."

The boys rode forward as the stranger waited on the trail. Tommy's heartbeat picked up, and he felt a nervousness in his stomach. He wondered if the stranger was a lawman. He couldn't see much of the man, as he wore a long, brown drover's coat and had his horse facing the two oncoming riders.

Closer, Tommy noticed that the man's horse was a flecked grey with dark ears. The man himself wore a dusty black hat. He had a bushy dark mustache, and the greying hair at his temples reached to his ears. He was not a large man, even with the dustcoat.

The boys rode on, horse hooves thudding, and drew rein at about five yards from the man. Red's voice sounded loud as he said, "Howdy."

"Afternoon, boys. How's everything?" The stranger was relaxed, not stern at all as Tommy had expected. His coffee-colored eyes roved over the two young men and their horses.

Red's voice was still a little louder than it needed to be. "Everything's swell. How 'bout yourself?"

"Just fine." The stranger was wearing lightweight riding gloves, and he rested his hands on the saddle horn as he held his reins. "Name's Bill Lockwood," he said. "Just passin' through. Thought I'd stop and be cordial."

Tommy noticed the man's bedroll and duffel bag tied onto the back of his saddle. The man looked like a traveler, all right. Tommy waited for Red to speak.

"You bet. I'm Red Armstrong, and this is my pal, Tommy Reeves. We work for Vinch Cushman and the White Wings Ranch."

Lockwood nodded. "Pleased to meet you. Your outfit is over that way, isn't it?"

"That's right. We've got a few minutes, so we thought we'd drop over to the Mexican camp. Water our horses and say hello."

"No harm in that."

"You know them?"

"Not yet." Lockwood glanced to his left and beyond Tommy. "How far is it to Fenton?"

Red tipped his head up and to the right. "About ten miles. Mostly south."

"About what I thought." Lockwood touched the brim of his hat. "Well, I'll move along. Good meetin' you boys. Maybe we'll see you again sometime." He backed his horse away to the side, and a rifle and scabbard came into view.

"Same to you," Red answered. "Good luck."

"Same here," said Tommy. "Nice to meet you, and good luck."

The boys rode on for a quarter of a mile without speaking. A jackrabbit sprang up from behind a clump of sagebrush and bolted away, zigzagging twice before it disappeared over a low rise.

Red spoke. "Is he gone?" After a couple of seconds he added, "I mean this fellow Lockwood."

"Oh." Tommy turned in his seat and looked back. The grey horse and dark rider made a small figure heading southward. "Yeah, he's gone."

Red let out a breath. "Huh." He moistened his lips. "What do you think he is?"

"I don't know. Like he said. Someone passin' through."

"I wonder if he's a stock detective. You know, some of them wear a dark coat or a dark slicker. Better for night work."

"Did you think he looked like one?"

Red laughed. "I don't know what they're supposed to look like. If I ever met one, I didn't know it. Just like right now."

"Maybe he is one."

Red gave another laugh. "Then we'd better watch our *p*'s and *q*'s."

An image of a lone, reddish-brown animal passed through Tommy's mind. "No need to do any more of that stuff."

Red stuck the tip of his tongue out of the corner of his mouth. "Nah. Especially with girls to look out for."

They rode at an easy lope until they came to the crest of a hill in the rolling country. A light breeze met them as they stopped the horses for a breather. Ahead of them where the ground sloped away, close to a stream that wound its way through the grassland, sat a group of low wooden buildings.

Red rubbed the back of his hand across his nose. "There it is," he said. "Little Mexico. Just remember, be on your best behavior. All we want to do is water our horses — and take a look around. I don't think anyone will start a fight, but if they do, try not to go along with it."

Tommy's stomach was feeling nervous again. "I won't. I haven't been in a fight since I left home, and I don't want to start now. Especially here."

As they rode down the slope at a walk, Tommy had time to take in various details. The little settlement consisted of a huddle of wooden houses with a lane running through the middle. Goats wandered about. A grey burro came into view. Clothes hung on a clothesline with chickens pecking at the ground nearby. A group of five children sent out a laughing sound as they ran around and played. Two dogs, one light-colored and one dark, came to the edge of the village and began barking.

An older boy came out of one of the houses and quieted the dogs. He stood waiting, and a man with dark hair and no hat appeared in the doorway that the boy had come out of. The man stood in the shadow until Red and Tommy rode to the edge of the village, and then he came forward in the sunlight.

"Good afternoon," he said.

"Afternoon," Red called back. He and Tommy stopped their horses.

Tommy nodded at the boy, who leaned forward, smiling, as he held the collars of the two dogs.

"How can I help you?" asked the man.

Red answered. "We'd like to water our horses if we could."

The man nodded. He pointed toward a

wooden trough where a dull brown horse with thin hindquarters stood motionless. "Over there."

Red swung his right leg over the saddle horn and the horse's neck, and he slid off to the ground. "Appreciate it," he said. "My name's Red."

The man gave a nod of the head. "Raimundo Villarreal, at your service."

Tommy swung down in normal fashion, nodded at the man, and followed Red to the water trough.

The dull brown horse moved away. Red loosened the cinch on his saddle, and Tommy did likewise. As the two ranch horses drank, Raimundo joined the group and stood a couple of yards away.

"Do you work for Cooshmon?" he asked.

"That's right," Red answered.

"Well, we don't want any trouble."

Red put on a wide smile. "You won't get any from us. We like to be friends."

"I don't think your boss does. He doesn't like us." Raimundo's eyes settled on Tommy. "And you? You're just a young boy."

Beyond the man, Tommy saw a girl appear in the doorway. He felt as if he was standing next to himself and hearing himself speak. "I like to be friends, too. Or we wouldn't have come here."

"Well, you look like good boys. But you gotta watch out for your boss. He doesn't like us, and if he catches you comin' here, he might give you hell, too."

Red cut in. "We can take care of that."

Raimundo addressed Tommy again. "What's your name?"

"Tommy."

"That's good." Raimundo put his hand on Tommy's shoulder. "Be careful. You look like a good boy, and I don't want you to get into any trouble. But for friends, you are welcome here." The man's eyes had a kindly expression as he nodded affirmation.

"Thanks." Tommy offered his hand, and they shook. Then as Raimundo shook hands with Red, Tommy caught another glance at the girl standing in the doorway.

Red broke the silence. "You've got somethin' like a little town here."

"A village," said Raimundo. "We are eight families here, or eight houses. You say homes?"

"Households."

"Oh, yeah. Well, each one has a claim of a hundred sixty acres, but we come together here. We look out for each other."

"That's good." Red's glance was wandering around. He came back to the group and said, "Are you all kin? Like family to one another?"

"Some by blood, some by marriage. Alejo and I are married to sisters. And he has two nephews. That's four houses. And so on. Just one incomplete one. My wife's cousin, José Acevedo, he died young. So his wife and kids, they're a house."

"I see. Who has the sheep? Or do you all have?"

"We run the animals together. Well, you know, the goats, they go where they want."

"Looks like the donkeys do, too."

"The burros? Oh, they're all right. They're good when we need 'em."

"You outfit your sheep camps with 'em, huh?"

"Yeah. That's right."

Red's gaze wandered again.

Raimundo said, "We don't have much, but we hope to grow."

Red's voice sounded vacant as he said, "Sure."

Raimundo turned to Tommy. "You don't talk much."

"Not at first. I'm just listenin', learnin' things."

"That's a good way."

"I was wondering about one thing, though. Aren't you supposed to live on your claim?"

17

"Oh, yeah. And do improvements. Build a house, dig a well. But you can't do it all at once. We're just gettin' started. But we got a shack on every claim, and someone stays there when they got the sheep there. That's the sheep camps."

"And you stay together here because this is where you got water?"

"That's right."

Tommy looked around and saw where the land sloped down to the creek. "You've got good water here."

"We just barely touch it in this one place, maybe a hundred yards. But it's good."

Red came back into the conversation. "Are you people Spanish or are you Mexican?"

"We call ourselves *la gente*. The people. We all born here. My family goes back to Spain. We're not Indian. But we're Mexican because where we come from, over there in New Mexico Territory, it used to be Mexico."

Tommy's eyes traveled back to the doorway where the girl had been standing. A second girl had joined her, and the two of them were talking. Tommy was trying to think of a way to ask about the girls when the scene was interrupted. A well-dressed man with a full head of shiny hair and a trimmed mustache walked past the girls and said something. The girls went into the house, and the man walked forward in Raimundo's direction. Tommy figured him to be about thirty or a little less. He wouldn't be a father to the girls, but he might be a bossy older brother. He had an air of importance about him as he held his head high and did not speak to Red or Tommy. Rather, he swept them with a dark glance and gave them the shoulder as he said something in Spanish to Raimundo.

The older man answered with a tone and an expression suggesting that he already knew whatever the well-groomed man was saying. At this point the boy, who had been making himself inconspicuous all the while, took off in the direction of the house. The well-dressed man turned and walked away in the opposite direction.

Raimundo said, "My son has to go for a burro. He steps over the fence and eats the green of the onions."

Red found his opening. "I thought that was your son. He looks like you. Good-looking boy. Were those your daughters?"

"One is my daughter, the other my niece. Alejo's daughter."

"Oh, so they're cousins."

"Sure." Raimundo gave the impression that he had spoken as much as he cared to about the girls. He looked over the two ranch horses and said, "You boys ride a long ways in a day?"

"Sometimes," said Tommy.

"Well, you wanna visit again sometime, you welcome here."

"Thanks." Tommy led his horse out a couple of steps, pulled the cinch, and tightened it.

Red did the same. He looked over his shoulder to smile at Raimundo, then swung himself up into the saddle without sticking his foot in the stirrup. He gigged his horse and tipped his hat. As he moved away, Tommy poked his toe in the stirrup and swung aboard in the usual way. He waved his hand at Raimundo and touched his heel to the horse.

The girls were nowhere in sight. Tommy waited until he and Red were well beyond the edge of the village, and then he looked back to see if the girls had come out the back door. All he saw was clothes on a clothesline, moving in the light breeze. So much for wishful thinking. But Raimundo had invited them to drop by again some time. It seemed like a good idea.

Tommy hung his hat on a peg and stretched out on his bunk, hands behind his head. He watched Red drink water from a tin cup, and he started when the bunkhouse door opened. Tommy settled down when he saw that it was Walt McKinney.

"Hello, boys," Walt said. "Did you just get in?"

Red shook the drops out of the tin cup and said, "A few minutes ago. We just put our horses away. Anything new?"

"Nah." Walt took off his hat and hung it next to Tommy's. As he turned around, the imperfect light in the bunkhouse gave him a gaunt appearance. He was lean and of average height, with curly blond hair and a narrow chin. He gave a tight smile as he turned a chair away from the table and sat down. He took a breath with his mouth open, and his small teeth showed. "Another day, another dollar." He reached into his vest pocket and drew out a small white sack of tobacco and a pack of papers.

He shook tobacco into a leaf of paper he held troughed with his thumb and fingers, then pulled the yellow drawstring with his teeth. He tossed the bag to Red, who caught it with one hand as he pulled a chair around for himself. McKinney rolled the cigarette he had begun and licked the seam. Pausing before he put the cigarette in his mouth, he asked, "See anything?" Then he flipped the cigarette to his lips and popped a match.

"Jackrabbit," Red answered. Sitting relaxed in the chair, he pushed back his hat and began to roll a cigarette.

Walt blew out a stream of smoke and said, "That's about the way it is."

Red finished rolling his cigarette and motioned to Walt for a match.

The bunkhouse door opened again, and Tommy's pulse jumped with good reason. Lew Greer, the foreman, filled the doorway, and Vinch Cushman followed right behind.

Red blew smoke toward the ceiling, turned his head, and said, "Howdy."

"Don't howdy me," said Greer. He was a bulky man, and his broad-brimmed hat cast his face in shadow.

Red sat up straight and kept his composure. "What's wrong?"

Greer gave an expression of disgust. "As if you didn't know."

"I'll have to say I don't."

"No need to act dumb," Greer said. "You were over at the Mexican camp, the two of you."

Red blinked his eyes. "Never said we weren't."

"Don't get smart. You asked what's wrong, and I'm tellin' you. There's no reason to go over there and mingle with those people."

"We just went to water our horses."

"Oh, go on. It's well over a mile out of your way." Greer held up a thick hand and wagged his finger. "We don't need any of that."

"I didn't know there was anything wrong with it."

"You don't know much." Greer spit tobacco juice into the spittoon.

Red shrugged, as if he didn't have anything more to say. He raised his cigarette to his lips, and Greer batted it away.

"Pay attention when I'm talkin'."

Red settled his hat on his head and spoke in an apologetic tone. "I was listening. I just didn't know what to say. I didn't expect anyone to be mad."

Vinch Cushman's deep voice filled the room. "You kids are young and don't know any better. But we're tellin' you. Stay away from those people. They're no good. They breed like rats." Cushman turned to glare at Tommy. The boss had one eye wider than the other, and his complexion was flushed. "Are you listening?"

Tommy sat up on his bunk and made himself look straight at the boss. "Yes, I am," he said.

Cushman loomed over him from ten feet away. The man had hunched and rounded shoulders, a head that leaned forward, and a beak nose. He reminded Tommy of a bird of prey. His voice took command again. "You need to understand. These people aren't the same as us. They're a lower class. Bad enough that they run sheep, but they've got a poor way of doin' things. Just look at the way they manage. Bang any kinds of boards together to make a shed. Tie their corrals together with old broken pieces of rope. You won't find any cattleman worth his salt who does things that way. Like a rat's nest. But that's the way they are." Vinch flared his nostrils as he took a big sniff. "The cattlemen were here first, by God. We opened this country up, did all the hard work, and now these rag-tails come in and squat on our range."

Greer picked up on the topic. "Rag-tail is right. Like their horses — what horses they got. Broomtail, skinny-ribbed, miserable things with their heads hangin' low and their hip bones stickin' out. Granger horses. Any self-respectin' cow outfit would cull out that kind of horse, take 'em to the boneyard, and put a bullet in their head."

Tommy flinched.

Cushman spoke again in his deep voice. "You kids don't know any better, and that's why we're explainin' it to you. I can tell by the way both of you look at me that you don't believe me. Maybe you don't think I know what I'm talkin' about."

"I wouldn't say that," Red answered.

"Don't even think it," said Greer. "Listen to men who know better. I'll tell you, I been around Mexicans plenty, and I know. Fact is, I know them better than they know themselves." Greer seemed to have reached a point at which he was satisfied with himself and could afford to be tolerant of his inferiors. "Go pick up your cigarette," he said.

As Red moved out of the way, Tommy saw that Fred Berwick, the fourth puncher at the White Wings Ranch, had come in behind the boss and the foreman. Fred was looking on in an uneasy way, as if he didn't want to be siding with the boss but didn't have the power to differ with him.

Cushman's voice broke the silence. "I'll just say one thing. I know what I'm talkin' about." He must have followed Tommy's eyes, for he turned and made a small hand gesture. "And Fred knows I do. Isn't that right, Fred?"

Greer laughed. "Fred don't want to say. But, of course, he knows it. Don't you, Fred?"

Fred stood with his thumbs in his belt and

nodded.

Red picked up his cigarette and took a puff on it. He motioned with his head, raising his hat brim, and said, "Have you got another match, Walt?"

McKinney reached into his vest and came out with a match. He struck it on the side of his chair, and it sputtered into a flame. As Red leaned toward it, Cushman's voice rose again.

"You two kids need to bring in some stove wood. Walt, you help Fred with whatever he needs. Fred, you're in charge of the kitchen, of course. Just go easy on the salt."

Fred nodded and said, "Sure."

Tommy stayed out of the way as he rose from his bunk and put on his hat. He slipped outside and waited for Red.

A moment later, Red stepped out of the bunkhouse. He paused to take one last pull on his cigarette, drop the snipe, and grind it out with the sole of his boot.

The boys walked to the woodpile without speaking. Once there, when they could see no one was within hearing distance, Red said, "I wonder who told on us."

Tommy said, "It could have been any of them, or Vinch could have seen us himself."

"Old Eagle Eye." Red made a small puffing sound. "Probably doesn't matter." He bent over and began picking up lengths of split firewood.

Tommy did the same. When he had an armload, he straightened up and waited for Red. "That was quite a blow-up," he said.

Red shrugged a shoulder. "I've had worse."

"I was wondering about one thing. It seems — I don't know if I should mention it."

"Go ahead."

"Do you think Vinch hates those people because they're not white?"

"Oh, I imagine so. Why do you ask?"

"It's the one thing he didn't mention."

"Probably goes without sayin'."

"And then Lew callin' 'em grangers. Not that it matters, I suppose, but grangers are dirt farmers. These small outfits that come in and cut the range into smaller pieces, they're called nesters. Not that it's any better of a term. But that's what I was told. Once you get straightened out on your language, you know, you don't like to hear the words used wrong."

"I know what you mean. Someone from the East, wearin' a derby hat, steps off the train and calls your gelding a stallion." Red shook his head. "Pity him."

CHAPTER TWO

Tommy sat in the shade of his horse, picking at the dry grass and watching the low hill where he expected Red to ride over. The air did not stir, and here at ground level, the temperature seemed hotter. Tommy guessed it had something to do with the sun's rays hitting the dry earth. He reached out beyond the shadow and touched the dirt between the clumps of buffalo grass. The soil was warm and dry, collecting the sun's heat. And yet the ants worked on through an afternoon like this, obedient to whatever laws they followed.

Tommy looked up to scan the countryside. He would have to be much closer to the crest of the hill in order to hear the hoofbeats before he saw the rider, especially on a hot day like this. Sound traveled better in cold weather, and even more so when there was snow on the ground. He was pretty sure of it. He had noticed it himself. No one had told him.

The thought of sounds in cold weather brought to mind the tall tales of Paul Bunyan. In the snowy forest, the camp cook would have five men holler all at once to shout a message to the next camp. At the other camp, the cook would have five men listening, with the logic that if five men could shout farther than one, five men could hear farther as well. Tommy wondered if anyone was ever expected to believe those tales.

When he thought of the Paul Bunyan stories, another one came to mind. The camp cook had a skillet so big that he made a boy like Tommy strap on two slabs of bacon, like skates, and skim all around the surface to grease it for flapjacks. When Tommy thought of that tale, he wondered what would happen if the boy fell down. He would get a bad burn. That was never part of the story, though. The boy just skated on a lake of hot grease.

Here came Red now, on the dark horse he had saddled that morning. Tommy did not hear the hoofbeats yet. Sound traveled slower than sight. He knew that, too. Once when he was working at the Muleshoe, he watched from about four hundred yards as one of the other riders shot a deer. The rifle kicked, the deer fell over, and the sound carried a couple of seconds later.

Now Tommy heard the hooves striking the earth, and he saw bits of dust rising. He stood up, brushed off the seat of his pants, and waited.

The horse slowed and came to a stop, its breath heaving and its warmth spreading out. Red took off his hat and wiped his brow with his shirtsleeve. His copper-colored hair glared in the sun. He put his hat back on and said, "Ready, kid?"

Tommy squinted. "I don't know if we should."

Red let out an impatient breath. "Oh, come on now. This is the time to do it. Every three days, we finish up over here. This is the closest we get."

"I don't know if we should today."

"Well, if we're going to do it, we might as well do it now. We can wait three days and decide again, but that'll just be three days wasted. What do you want, anyway?"

"I want to get to know one of those girls. You know that." Tommy looked around on both sides. "I'm just worried about what might happen."

"You mean Vinch? All he can do is get mad. He's already done that, and it looked to me like he cooled down. Besides, there's no guarantee that he'll find out, and if he does, he can get over it."

"I don't know."

"Look. Sooner or later, we're gonna go back. If you don't want to, I'll go by myself. I know he doesn't like it. But I'm not gonna sit over here all my life, with girls over there, and not even get a chance to meet 'em, just because someone else doesn't like it."

An image of the girl with dark hair passed through Tommy's mind, as it had done a hundred times in the last three days. "I know," he said. "But —"

"But what? You want to be like Fred Berwick all your life? Faint heart never won a fair maid. You know that."

Tommy smiled. "Yeah, I know." He moved the horse around, set his reins in place, and grabbed the saddle horn. The horse stepped forward, and Tommy snugged the near rein. When the horse moved backward, Tommy put his foot in the stirrup and swung aboard.

"That's a sport." Red made a clucking sound and touched his spur to the dark horse. The two riders moved out together.

The board village caught the sun just as it had done a few days earlier. The weathered lumber gave off a dull shine. Laundry hung on the clothesline, chickens pecked at the earth, and a brown-and-white goat wandered across the bare ground. Two dogs came out to bark, and a girl appeared at the doorway that Tommy kept an eye on. His pulse quickened.

The girl called to the dogs, but they kept barking. The girl went inside. A minute later, Raimundo appeared. He spoke to the dogs, and they trotted back to him, wagging their tails.

The chickens and the goat drifted away as the boys rode into the yard. They stopped within ten yards of Raimundo and dismounted. All three exchanged greetings as they shook hands.

"We eat dinner a little bit late today," Raimundo said. "Come and eat."

"Oh, no," said Red. "We don't want to interrupt anything."

Tommy felt his hopes sinking.

"Oh, no, you eat," said Raimundo. "My son will water your horses, and we will eat. And talk." The man gave a nod of encouragement and an inviting gesture with his hand.

Raimundo's son came out of the house, and the father spoke to him in Spanish. The boy smiled and took the reins of the two horses. Red and Tommy followed Raimundo into the house.

Tommy's eyes took a minute to adjust to the dim interior. At the far end of the front room, a table sat next to a doorway that led into the kitchen. A matronly woman in a dark dress and a pale apron stood at a cook-stove, and the aroma of cooked food wafted through the doorway.

"Sit down," said Raimundo.

Of the four chairs around the table, Tommy took the one that faced the kitchen doorway. He took off his hat and kept it in his lap as he sat down. Red did the same. Tommy saw that only one empty chair remained. He met Raimundo's eyes and said, "I don't think there's going to be enough room."

"Don't worry," said the host. "The others will eat later. It's the way we do things."

The table had not been set. Something like a jar or vase, made of clay, sat in the middle of the table with forks and spoons sticking out of it. A small wooden burro with panniers of woven grass held a supply of toothpicks, and next to it sat a low, round dish made of glazed clay and half-full of a reddish sauce.

Motion caught Tommy's eye, and a current ran through him. A girl with long, dark hair and a reddish-brown dress came out of the kitchen with a tan crockery plate of cooked food and set it in front of Raimundo. She said something in Spanish, and Tommy caught the word *"papá."* As she returned to the kitchen, passing again behind Red's chair, Tommy admired her dark hair, straight and neat and clean as it lay on her shoulders and upper back.

She reappeared in another minute with a plate for Red. She made a quick return to the kitchen, and Tommy sat up straight and held his breath until she came back out with a plate for him. He exhaled slow and silent, waiting to see if her eyes would meet his. They did. She had dark eyes, deep and shiny, that settled on him for a second and moved away.

"Thank you," he said.

"You're welcome."

He was so dazed that he missed seeing her walk away. He came back to himself and the table and the meal. Red was lifting a fork out of the clay jar, and Raimundo was watching the kitchen doorway. The middle-aged woman Tommy had noticed earlier came out of the kitchen with a small bundle wrapped in a towel. She set it in the middle of the table.

"Tortillas," she said.

Tommy looked at his plate. He had a full meal of scrambled eggs, mashed beans, and fried pork. He waited for Raimundo to take a tortilla. He took one for himself, warm and white with brown toasted spots. As he reached for a fork, he saw that Raimundo had torn off a piece of tortilla and was using it in place of a utensil. Tommy went ahead and took a fork from the vase.

"Here's *chile*," said the host. He lifted a spoon from the vase and stuck it in the bowl of sauce.

Red shook his head.

Tommy shrugged and decided to give it a try. He served a spoonful of the red sauce onto the beans. He put the spoon back in the bowl, got set with the tortilla in one hand and the fork in the other, and dug in.

The meal was sensational. After weeks of the same bunkhouse fare of fried potatoes, fried salt pork, boiled beans with bacon rind, and rock-hard biscuits, the Mexican food had spark and variety. Tommy could not remember the last time he had eaten eggs, and even the fried pork had some other spice that perked things up.

"This food is wonderful," he said. "Incredible."

Red chimed in. "You bet."

"This is the good life," said Raimundo. "Maybe we don't have much money, or a very fancy house, but the Mexican people, we always have the good food." He smiled. "We are happy people. Even when we have only beans and chile, we enjoy our food and we are thankful to God."

"Amen," said Red.

Tommy paused. He couldn't help thinking that Red's sincerity was at least equaled by his interest in the girl who had served the plates of food.

Raimundo went on. "And this is the good thing, that we sit down in friendship."

"It's very good," said Tommy. He searched for the words and found them. "We didn't expect it. But we appreciate it."

"It's my pleasure." Raimundo reached for another tortilla. "And yet, maybe we will not be friends for very long."

"Why's that?" asked Red.

"Your boss, Mr. Cooshmon, he does not like us."

"I know," Red answered. "You told us that last time."

"Oh, no. There is more now."

"Really?" said Tommy. "What is it?"

"He tells us we should leave."

"Leave?" Tommy frowned. "You've filed claims, haven't you?"

"Oh, yes. But he doesn't care. He says that if we don't leave, he will cut off our water. And if we don't leave after that, there will be other consequences."

Red cleared his throat and said, "When did all this happen? After we were here the last time?"

"Yes. Day before yesterday. He came over here with the other man. The one we call *El Gordo*. The fat one."

"That's Lew. His name's Lew Greer."

Raimundo shrugged.

Tommy met his gaze and said, "What do you think you'll do, then?"

Raimundo raised his eyebrows. "Well, we don't just pack up and leave because of something he says. We have to wait and see what he does."

'Do you think he'll cut off your water?"

"I don't know. But we don't see any good in him. He has a bad eye. It's what the people call *mal ojo*. He can look at a baby or a weak person, and he can make them sick, give them a bad spirit."

"Like a curse?" Tommy said.

"That's it."

Red sniffed. "There's bad blood, all right."

"Yeah? We think so. That's why I say maybe we don't be friends for very long."

Tommy said, "Well, this isn't going to turn us against you."

"No," said Raimundo. "But he is a very hard man. And probably he will not let you come here anymore. Maybe you say different, but he's the boss."

Red pushed away his empty plate. "Well, I'm sorry to hear all of this. It doesn't sound good to me."

"Some things you cannot change," said Raimundo. "Maybe you don't come back. Maybe you come back but not for a long time. We don't know the future. But we are friends today. That is the only reason I invite you to eat in my house."

Tommy said, "I'm glad you told us about him trying to make you leave."

"I don't want you boys to get in trouble with your boss."

Red gave a short laugh. "Sooner or later, it'll be hard not to be in trouble with him. Like you said, he's a hard man. From what you just told us, he's harder than I realized."

"I don't think he'd do anything to you boys, but be careful."

Red took a breath. "Oh, we will."

Tommy had a sense that the conversation had run its course and served its purpose. He cleaned up his plate and set it aside. "Well," he said, "we sure thank you for the meal. And I hope we get to come back again before long."

"If God wishes it." Raimundo smiled.

Red scooted back his chair and stood up.

"And please give our thanks to your wife. And your daughter, I guess."

"Thank you."

Tommy looked around, and seeing nothing of the womenfolk, he stood up as well. Raimundo accompanied them to the door, where he shook hands with each of them and said, "Just remember. You are always welcome here." They thanked him, put on their hats, and went outside.

Tommy blinked a couple of times as he adjusted to the brightness. He located their two horses and the boy who held the reins. The boy led the horses forward and handed the first set of reins to Tommy.

"Thank you," said Tommy. "What's your name?"

"Gabriel."

"Mine's Tommy. And this is Red."

The boy smiled and shook hands with each of them. Tommy figured him to be fourteen or fifteen.

Movement caught Tommy's attention. In the shade of the next house over, two girls stood talking. They were the same two he had seen on the first visit — the girl who had served their meal and the one who was her cousin.

Tommy brought his eyes back to meet Ga-

39

briel's. "Is that your sister, the one on the left?"

"Yes."

"What's her name?"

The boy looked down, and in a low voice he said, "Anita."

"Thanks." Tommy shook his hand again and said, "I don't think anyone will get in trouble if you just tell her my name."

The boy kept his eyes toward the ground, and shrugging, he said, "Probably not."

"Good. Just to be sure, I'll tell you again. It's Tommy."

"I know."

Red's voice was louder than the other two as he said, "Don't leave me out."

Tommy gave a light frown and made a gesture with his hand to suggest that Red keep his voice low. Back to Gabriel, he said, "And your cousin?"

The boy's voice was just above a whisper. "Elsa."

"Tell her Red thinks she's pretty."

Red let out a breath of exasperation. "I can speak for myself."

Tommy laughed. "Like Miles Standish?"

Gabriel gave them both a questioning look.

Red turned to the boy. "You can tell her my name. Red. And of course I think she's pretty. But don't tell her that if it's going to cause any trouble. Especially if it's going to make her father mad. Or any big brother."

Gabriel nodded in agreement, and the two visitors led their horses into the clear to mount up. Tommy waited to see if Red was going to perform his flying mount, but he didn't. He stepped into the stirrup and swung his leg over. Tommy did the same. He tipped his hat to the girls, waved, and rode away. Red held back a second, and Tommy imagined he wanted the stage to himself.

A minute later, Red caught up. He said, "Why did you tell him to say that?"

"What? That you thought his cousin was pretty?"

"Why did you say that? It put him and me both on the spot."

Tommy laughed. "I was just trying to help."

"Funny way of doing it."

Tommy evened his reins and smiled to himself. If he didn't help his own cause, no one else was going to.

Fred Berwick and Walt McKinney were sorting beans when Tommy and Red walked into the bunkhouse. Fred looked up and said, "Hello, boys."

Walt turned in his chair and tipped his ash in a sardine can. "Long ride today?"

"Same as usual," Red answered.

Tommy noticed the care with which Fred picked up a rotted, shriveled bean and set it to the side with the dirt clods, tiny rocks, and other bad beans.

Walt rubbed the underside of his stubbled chin and went back to sorting beans.

"Need any stove wood?" Red asked.

Fred shook his head. "I think we're all right."

Red cupped his hand on the back of his neck and stretched. "Would you like some help sortin' beans?"

"We're pretty close to done." Fred pursed his lips, and after a couple of seconds he said, "I expect Lew to be back in here in a few minutes."

"Oh." Red raised his eyebrows and looked at Tommy. They hung their hats and were on their way to their bunks when the door opened behind them and pushed a wave of air into the room.

Lew Greer's voice was loud and commanding. "I need to talk to you boys."

They turned around to face the foreman. He moved close, within arm's distance. Light from the doorway cast him in shadow, so that his stubbled face and glaring eyes

42

had the qualities of a storm ready to break open. A couple of specks of saliva flew as he said, "You two brats have a lot to learn."

Tommy looked from the foreman to Red, and he felt that something bad was about to happen.

Red's eyes narrowed, and his face tightened. He said, "I learn something every day."

"By listening to the Mexicans."

"That, too."

Greer's arm shot out, and he slapped Red on the cheekbone.

Red staggered aside, caught his balance, and stood with his fists at his side.

Greer planted his feet and held his fist at his side like a hammer. "Don't even think about it," he said. "For one thing, I'd beat you like a dog." The big man's face spread in a sneer of disapproval. "For another, you don't work here anymore." He turned his head so that he took in Tommy as well. "Neither of you. You don't work here, you don't live here, you don't do anything here. Pack your things, both of you." Greer's eyes narrowed, and his chest went up and down. "Sneakin' little sons of bitches, both of you. Well, let me tell you this. When you work for someone, you take orders. If you don't, you're nothin'." His voice slowed down.

"That's what you are. Nothin'. You've got an hour to pack your things and get gone. You step foot on any part of this ranch again, and you'll wish you hadn't."

"We've got pay comin'," said Red.

"You'll get it." Greer turned and lumbered out of the bunkhouse, pulling the door hard behind him.

Tommy looked at Fred and Walt. He imagined they were glad to have beans to sort.

Fred looked up and said, "Sorry, boys. Lew and Vinch are on a rampage."

"It's all right," Tommy said. "We did it to ourselves."

Red's voice came out with something of a quaver. "I'll tell you, that's the last time he'll ever hit me."

Walt twisted his mouth and said, "The less you make of any of this, the better." He went back to pushing beans.

Tommy noticed, as he had observed in the past, that Walt's fingernails were worn down to the pink, and the tips of his fingers grew beyond them. Tommy had never seen Walt chewing his nails, but he knew the signs.

Fred scrunched his nose. Without looking away from his work, he said, "It's better not to make a fuss. Take your pay and go quietly. That's what I'd do."

Red's voice was calm as he said, "I didn't mean today."

Fred nodded. "I know."

Tommy started packing his belongings. He didn't have much, just his war bag, his bedroll, and his rifle. Red had close to the same. In less than ten minutes, they were ready to go. They decided to saddle their horses and come back for their gear.

The sun was going down as they stepped outside. Tommy was thinking of his horse, an older animal that had been getting plenty of rest as Tommy was riding ranch horses. Older horses could still buck, though, and Tommy hoped Pete hadn't gotten too fresh.

As it turned out, Pete was calm as ever. He stood still as Tommy brushed and saddled him and checked his hooves. Tommy decided to climb aboard before he tied on all his gear, so he rode Pete from the barn to the bunkhouse. Pete was still a model of good behavior.

Inside the bunkhouse, Fred pointed at the two white tobacco sacks sitting on the edge of the table near the pile of beans. "Lew left these," he said. "One for each of you." Fred squinted as he went back to sorting.

Tommy picked up the nearer bag and felt the weight of coins. He put the bag in his pocket.

"Aren't you going to count it?" asked Walt.

"I can tell by the heft." In truth, he didn't think anyone would try to beat him out of his wages, and even if someone did, he didn't think it would do any good to complain. So it was easy to make a good show.

Red tucked away his bag in similar fashion. The boys shook hands with the other two punchers, then walked out into the dusk.

Tommy had an empty feeling as he led his horse away and climbed aboard. He thought it was strange that a chapter in life could end so fast, but he couldn't imagine how things could have worked out any different. Once he had seen Anita up that close, it was just a matter of time before he would have to ride away from the White Wings Ranch.

Night had drawn in when Tommy and Red rode into the town of Fenton. Light spilled out of the doorway of the Silver Bit saloon. Closer, Tommy heard piano music and men's voices.

"Looks like the café's still open," he said. "I don't know if you want to get anything to eat. I'm still all right after everything we ate at the Mexican camp."

"I don't need anything. Grub, that is."

"Shall we just go ahead and see if we can put up at the livery?"

"Might as well. I think I'll go in here for a minute first." Red stopped his horse in front of the saloon. "Get us some snakebite medicine."

Tommy felt a tenseness run through him. He and Red did not have an agreement, but they were as good as partners, stuck in this situation together. If Red drank, any problems that came up were Tommy's as well. He would have to stay on his toes. He knew that much. It was what kids got stuck with.

Tommy stayed mounted and held the reins of the other horse while Red went into the saloon. A couple of minutes later, Red came out through the swinging doors with a pint of whiskey in his hand. He put it in his saddlebag, took his reins from Tommy, and stepped up into the saddle.

Two blocks later, they dismounted at the livery stable. They made arrangements to board the horses for the night and to sleep in the straw for another two bits each. Full darkness had settled in by the time they put their horses away, and the lantern in the harness room cast a weak glow from a distance. Tommy and Red leaned back in the straw as Red twisted the stopper out of the bottle.

"Well, here's to it," he said as he held up the bottle and brought it to his lips. He took a moderate sip and lowered the bottle. "It's not the first time I've been out on the street, and I don't suppose it'll be my last."

"Same with me," said Tommy.

"I'll tell you, though. I'd rather be out of a job than takin' orders from someone like Lew Greer."

"I think that's what they call making a virtue out of necessity."

"I don't know as many big words as some people do."

"Neither do I."

"Well, here's what I think."

Tommy waited as Red took another sip.

"I think it probably saved us some trouble, gettin' fired like that."

"Could very well be."

"But it was still a high-handed thing to do. They did it because they could. Greer, he just likes to rub your nose in it. But he wouldn't do it if Vinch didn't want him to."

"Maybe not."

"Vinch is the son of a bitch. You remember all the stuff he said the other night, about being cattlemen and being here first? He really does think he's high and mighty."

"They think they've earned it."

"They think they own everything. They

think they've got a right to push anyone around. But they're not as smart as they think."

Tommy could see that Red was warming to the whiskey, and he decided not to feed the fire. So he said nothing.

"It would serve 'em right if someone pulled a little move on 'em."

Tommy frowned. He had an inkling of what Red meant. "Like what?" he asked.

"They wouldn't know about it. Be better if no one else did." Red's features relaxed as he smiled. "Just to show we could do it. Never leave a trace."

Tommy shook his head. "I think it would be better to leave that alone."

"Oh, it's just somethin' to think about. Nothin' we have to do if we don't want. But the chance is always there. Just knowin' you could do it is a good joke."

"I'd rather find something else to laugh at, not to mention something better to think about."

Red took another drink. "To tell you the truth, I would, too." His eyelids drooped as he nodded.

"Then I've got a good idea of what we can do tomorrow."

CHAPTER THREE

The boys rode into the Mexican settlement from the south instead of from the west as before, and the sun hung overhead at midday. The change of perspective, in addition to the presence of people outside, made the place seem less sleepy and relaxed than on the first two visits. Tommy saw right away that Anita and her cousin Elsa were stirring a laundry tub that hung over a low fire. Gabriel was hoeing weeds in a small garden enclosed by a battered wire fence. Out in the open, not far from the water trough, a man was combing a shiny bay horse that had a white blaze and four white socks.

The man wore a straw hat, a drab cotton shirt, and faded denim trousers. On second glance, Tommy recognized him as the man who had spoken to the girls and had told Raimundo about the stray burro. In plainer clothes with his belly sagging, he did not carry himself with as much authority as before. All the same, he saw fit to turn his back on the boys as he groomed the horse.

The girls turned from their work and gave friendly glances, but Tommy sensed that they were inhibited by the other man's presence. Only Gabriel seemed unaffected. He climbed over the fence and walked forward with the hoe on his shoulder.

"Hey, boys. You're back. You look like you're going somewhere."

Red tipped back his hat as his horse came to a stop. "It's not so much where we're goin' as where we're comin' from. We don't work for Cushman anymore."

Gabriel's eyes widened. "Huh! Did you quit?"

"No, we got fired."

"*¡Hombre!* I better go tell my father."

The girls were watching as Red hooked his right leg up and over the saddle horn and slid off the saddle into a standing position. Tommy did not have that maneuver rehearsed yet, so he dismounted in the regular way, swinging his leg up and over the gear tied onto the back of his saddle.

In what might have been otherwise a vacant moment, another person appeared. A woman in a dark blue dress and shoulder-length dark hair walked past the man combing his horse. Even from a distance, Tommy could see that they ignored each other. The woman walked with an impressive movement of her hips. Tommy guessed her to be at least ten years older than he was, and as such, she did not steal his interest. But he could see that she was a full woman. She waved to the two girls tending to the laundry and called out a greeting in Spanish. The girls spoke back in cheery tones. The woman spoke a shorter greeting to Gabriel as he went back to his work, and she went into the Villarreal household. Tommy looked at Red, and he was sure his friend had not missed the scene.

Raimundo emerged from in back of the house. He was wearing a battered brown hat, a collarless grey shirt, and greyish-brown canvas trousers. The front of his shirt and the lap of his pants had dust and bits of grass clinging to them. He looked over the boys and the horses as he walked forward.

When he stopped, he brushed himself off and said, "Surprised to see you again. You're not working over there anymore?"

"Nope. We got fired."

"*¡Válgame!* For coming over here?"

"I think that was it."

"Oh, that's no good. Like you said, he's got bad blood."

Red waved his hand. "Ah, it doesn't

52

bother us that much. As they say, I've been thrown out of better places."

Raimundo laughed. "We say, *De mejores bailes me han corrido.* They have chased me out of better dances."

"That's it." Red tossed a glance at the girls and came back. "Anyway, not havin' anything in particular to do, we thought we'd drop by and see if there's anything we could help you with."

"I don't think so. Not right now. We might have to dig a well. That's a hard job."

Red's eyebrows went up. "Oh, boy. I guess so, if you do it by hand. But a drillin' rig is expensive. And slow."

Tommy's gaze drifted to the two girls stirring the laundry and to Gabriel hoeing in the garden. If these people had their water shut off, they would be caught pretty short. He said, "Do you think you should be storing up water? If Cushman does what he said, it might be a while until you can get it back."

"That's true. But I don't know if he's going to do it."

"If he does, you might not have much time." Tommy glanced around the yard. Even the goats and chickens would get thirsty. "Why don't you let us help? We can carry enough water to fill up everything

53

you've got."

"Tommy's right," said Red. "We've got time for it. We've got nothin' else to do, and this way you won't be left high and dry."

Raimundo looked around. "I guess we could find some things to fill up."

Tommy caught another glimpse of the girls and liked the idea of them watching him work. "Sure," he said. "Anything you've got — buckets, barrels, washtubs."

Tommy poured the two buckets of water into the wooden tub and trudged over to stand in the shade of the house. The sun had moved west from straight overhead and was blazing in the hottest part of the day. The girls had rinsed the laundry, wrung it, and hung it out to dry. They had gone inside, and the only other person working in the hot sun was Red.

Tommy let his breath even out. Hauling two buckets of water, time after time, a hundred yards upslope, was taking its toll on him. He was hungry, tired, and sweaty. The amount of water he carried each time, seven or eight gallons, seemed to add very little to the overall total. He wondered how much these people would appreciate the water or be careful with it when they had a full supply with no effort on their part. He imagined the man with the nice-looking bay horse using twenty gallons to take a bath, then pitching the water to settle the dust. Tommy felt himself getting short-tempered. His stomach was empty. From the position of the sun, he figured it must be at least two hours past noontime.

He had turned his back to the house and was headed to the creek when he heard a voice behind him.

"It's time to eat."

Tommy could have dropped the buckets right there, but he made a slow turn and squared his shoulders. He needed to keep up a good image with Gabriel. "I'll put these in the shade," he said.

Inside the dim house, Red was already seated in the chair he had occupied the day before. Raimundo sat in his place, and Gabriel took the fourth chair. As Tommy sat down, he stole a glance at the kitchen door but did not see Anita. He sat up straight and took a steady breath. With his eyes adjusted to the interior of the house, he saw that Raimundo had a plate in front of him and had begun to eat. Red sat back with his head up, in an attitude of expectation.

Movement at the kitchen door made Tommy look around. Anita's mother appeared with two crockery plates and set one in front of Red and the other in front of her son. Less than a minute later, she brought a plate for Tommy. The sight of the food, plus the aroma, lifted his spirits. Half of the tan plate was covered with cubed meat in a dark reddish sauce, and the other half had a healthy portion of mashed beans.

Something sparked, and he realized that Anita had appeared at the corner of his vision. He sat up straight as before, taking notice of her dark hair, the white apron snugged at her waist, and the two small bundles she held, one in each hand.

"Tortillas," she said, catching his eye. She set one stack between Gabriel and Tommy and the other stack between Red and her father. Tommy hoped for another glance, but she gave no further expression as she returned to the kitchen.

Tommy helped himself to a spoon and tasted a piece of the meat with the red sauce. It was spicy but very satisfying. The anxiety brought on by hunger was going away. He took another bite, this time getting some beans on the spoon as well. The combination tasted perfect.

Gabriel flipped the cloth off the top of the bundle and revealed a stack of yellow tortillas.

Tommy identified the trace of corn as it

arose with the light steam. Of course. The yellow tortillas were smaller than the white ones. Gabriel motioned for him to take one. As he did, he asked, "What kind of meat is this?"

"Pig."

"Pork. And the sauce?"

"*Chile colorado.* Red chile. Do you like it?"

Tommy searched for the right word. "It's magnificent."

"Some people think it is too hot."

Tommy smiled and looked across the table. "How are you getting along, Red?"

Red waved his hand in front of his mouth. "A little warm, but just fine."

Raimundo said, "You boys gettin' pretty hungry, uh?"

Red put on his agreeable smile. "I was gettin' that way, but this takes care of it."

"Yeah," said the father. "We eat a little later than you do. In the cities, you people have the noon whistle. Twelve o'clock. With the Mexicans, everything closes from one to three."

"Siesta time."

"Not everyone takes a siesta, but they have time to go home and eat dinner. This is the big meal for us."

"It is for some white people, too."

57

Tommy flinched at the blunt use of language, but Raimundo didn't seem to notice.

Red went on. "Farmers, for example. Especially during harvest when they've got a crew, they'll put on a big feed at dinnertime, and then the crew works on till dark. Lots of farmers never miss a meal. They're back at the house for the dinner bell all three times every day."

Raimundo smiled. "The cowboys have to work too far away sometimes."

"That's right. Lots of times, it's a dog's lunch." Red looked at Gabriel and said, "That means no food at all." Back to Raimundo, he said, "And there's plenty of times you ride out, and your work takes you longer and farther than you thought."

"Oh, I know. I been a cowboy."

"It's not for everybody. And even if you like it, not every boss is a good one. We sure found that out."

"Oh, yeah. Cooshmon. The *zopilote.*"

Tommy paused with his spoon. "What's that?"

"The *zopilote*? He's the big bird." Raimundo hunched his head forward, held out his arms, and flapped them in slow motion. "A big, ugly bird, that eats dead things."

All the boys laughed, and Tommy said,

"The buzzard."

"*Ándale,*" said Raimundo. "That's him. *Zopilote. Buitre.*"

Red had his elbow on the table as he waved his spoon. "You've got two words for 'em? We do, too. Buzzard, vulture."

"I know those words," said Raimundo. "But that's what we call him, the boss."

Gabriel tore a corn tortilla in half as he repeated the word with a hard *s* and in four distinct syllables. *"Zopilote."*

Tommy found Gabriel's repetition interesting. It seemed like a habit or a matter of course, a way of affirming what the other person had said. At the same time, it sounded like a humorous word to pronounce. Tommy tried it in silence, and it made him smile.

The afternoon shadows were growing longer when Tommy set his buckets next to the house. Red had already taken a seat in the shade next to Raimundo, and the two of them were rolling cigarettes from a sack of Bull Durham that Red had bought in town that morning. A few of the other residents of the village were sitting outside as well. Tommy did not know how many of them had come out of their houses, which warmed up in the afternoon, and how many had come in from work. After carrying water all afternoon, he felt entitled to some of it, so he walked over to the trough and began splashing his face.

Gabriel showed up alongside him. "You going to spend the night here?"

"I don't know. Nobody has said anything." Tommy glanced at his and Red's horses, tied to the posts of a little shed where they had left their gear before they went to work. "One way or the other, we should water our horses."

"My father says you can sleep where you have your —" Gabriel seemed to grope for a term in English — "your saddles and things."

Tommy shrugged. "If no one else minds." The man who had been brushing the bay horse earlier had brought out a sleek white horse with freckles and was brushing it in the shade. In spite of the heat, the man was wearing dark pants, a dark jacket, a white shirt, and no hat. Tommy had the impression that the man had some kind of status he wanted to maintain, not only in the eyes of the other villagers but with any visitors as well. Tommy met Gabriel's eyes, gave a small tip of the head, and asked, "Who is that man?"

"His name is Faustino. Faustino Romero.

He is nephew to my uncle Alejo."

"I think your father mentioned that the other day. He's some kind of cousin of yours, then."

"Yes, but not a first cousin, as you say."

"Oh." Tommy wondered why it mattered.

"He has a brother. The two of them are very strong. In the town."

"I see. And they have families?"

"Emilio, the brother, has a wife and two little ones. But Faustino is still not married."

A light began to glow in Tommy's mind. "Do you remember a woman earlier in the day, who went into your house when you went to tell your father that Red and I were here?"

"Oh, yes. Milena."

Tommy glanced at Faustino and kept his voice low. "You know, I saw her walk past him, and I could swear that they both made a point of ignoring each other."

Gabriel shook his head. "Oh, no. They don't like each other anymore."

"They did at one time?"

"Milena, she's a widow. She has two little children. Faustino, he was single, and two or three years older. Everyone thought they should be together. She would be a good woman for him. So Faustino visits her on Sunday and all of that. But little by little he gets cold. And this is at the time that my sister Anita is going to be fifteen. You know, the celebration. She's going to be a *señorita*. And Faustino, all he can do is look at her. The other men say, oh, yeah, he wants something new. But he doesn't say anything. He doesn't talk to my father, he doesn't ask if he can come and visit on Sunday, he doesn't say anything to Anita. He just looks at her. Everybody knows."

Tommy took in a breath. "How old is he?"

"Maybe thirty."

"Is he afraid someone will say no?"

Gabriel scrunched his nose. "That is what people think."

"And Anita? If she could say for herself, what would she say?"

Gabriel seemed to become defensive, noncommittal. "I don't know. They are all older, and they know more than I do. And like the men say, you never know what a girl will accept."

With a slow turn of the head, Tommy observed Faustino Romero. The man gave off an aura of self-assurance, bordering on superiority. Tommy felt resentment welling up. *Better not,* he told himself. These people had their own rules, and he was an outsider. Rather than get worked up about someone else, he should tend to his own affairs.

"I think I'll water our horses," he said.

Gabriel nodded. "I have to go find ours."

Tommy untied the two horses and led them to the water trough. Again he had the clean feeling of deserving the water, as he had carried it. He let his thoughts wisp away as the horses lowered their muzzles into the water and caused little swirls as they drank.

The light sound of a female voice, not very close, caused him to raise his head and come back to the world around him. Anita and her cousin Elsa were carrying a sooty cauldron between them. It hung by the handle on an old broomstick that still had the stub of a head on Elsa's end. They hung the vessel on the tripod where the washtub had hung earlier. They walked back to the Villarreal house, in a motion worth watching, and Elsa came out with a white flour sack that was bulging full. It looked heavy as she carried it against her abdomen. Anita came out behind her, carrying two pails that were smaller than the ones Tommy had used. She dipped each one into the tub he had filled, and she followed her cousin to the fire pit. Elsa set the bag on the ground and took one pail from Anita. They poured the water into the cauldron and went to work on the bag. It was tied with a sack-sewer's stitch, with two ears sticking up. The girls unwound the string on one ear, pulled it out of the stitch across the top, and unwound the remaining wrap. Then, with each girl holding one ear, they lifted the sack and poured a stream of yellow corn into the large kettle.

Tommy pursed his lips. *They're going to boil corn.*

The horses were finished drinking, so he led them back by way of the outdoor fire. It wasn't a fire yet, however. The girls were poking scraps of old lumber beneath the belly of the cauldron, but only a thin trail of smoke drifted up. Elsa settled onto her knees and took up a foot-long board about eight inches wide and began waving air at the bed of coals. Only ashes rose.

Anita glanced at Tommy as he approached with the horses. She lowered her head and spoke to her cousin in Spanish. Tommy could not understand the words, but the tone was low, urgent, and girlish.

"Can I help?" he asked.

Anita did not look quite at him as she said, "We are trying to start this fire."

"Maybe I can do something." Holding the two lead ropes in one hand, he took off his hat and leaned toward the fire pit. He waved his hat several times, finding the right angle so as not to raise so many ashes. At last he saw a faint glow, a little more than a spark.

"Here," he said. "Can you hold these?" He handed the two lead ropes to Anita.

Elsa had stood up and moved back, so Anita stepped back as well and handed one of the ropes to her cousin.

Tommy put his hat on his head, took out his pocketknife, and knelt. He found a thin piece of lumber and began cutting off shavings. The knife slipped, and the pieces came off small, but that was all right. He blew life again into the little body of coals, then built a nest of shavings on top and blew again. A tiny flame jumped up, spread, and grew. He put in the larger shavings, then the rest of the stick. He split another thin piece into four spindles and laid them on. From there he built the fire with the wood that the girls had put in. Smoke poured out and up around the cauldron, and after a couple of minutes the fire burned cleaner.

Tommy rose up and stood back. He smiled at Anita as she handed him the two ropes. He looked around and saw Elsa walking toward the back of the Villarreal house.

"She's going to bring more wood," Anita said.

"That's good." After a couple of seconds of silence he said, "It looks like you're going to boil corn."

"Yes, we are. Thank you for helping."

"You're welcome." He took off his hat and fanned the air in a light motion. "By the way, my name's Tommy."

"I know. My brother told me."

"He said your name is Anita. That's a pretty name."

She blushed. "Thank you." A stick popped in the fire, and she started. She regained her composure and said, "You used to work for the big rancher."

"That's true. I did. But not any longer."

"My father says you are a young boy to be working alone, away from your family."

"Well, I'm sixteen. Some kids get a younger start than that. But I don't have much family."

"Oh."

From the tone of her voice he thought he had said something disagreeable, so he went on. "I have some family, but not real close. I was raised by my aunt and uncle. In eastern Nebraska. That's quite a ways from here."

"I know."

"But they had their own kids to raise, and my uncle didn't have a farm. He worked for other people. So I did, too. Farm work. I saved up enough money to go out on my own."

"And you came here."

"That's right. I came west on the train, and I went to work for a ranch out of Laramie. A place called the Muleshoe. I had to have my own coat and boots and saddle. It took all my money. But I worked for them through the fall and winter, and I saved enough money to buy an old horse. This one. His name's Pete."

Anita looked at the horse and smiled. "And then you went to work for Cushman?"

The name stung him. "I didn't know what kind of a man he was. But the Muleshoe didn't pay me a full wage, and he did. It was a bottom wage, but it was better." Tommy stared at the blaze. "I know how to work. That's the good thing. I'll get another job and keep working my way up."

Anita stared at the fire as well. The light reflected on her face and made her eyes shine. "That's good, that a boy knows how to work. My father makes my brother work all the time."

Tommy wished she wouldn't rank him as a boy, but if she saw herself as just a girl, maybe it wasn't bad. "And you?" he asked.

"Oh, he makes me work, too. After we boil this corn, my brother will grind it, and my cousin and I will make tortillas."

"You do other work as well. You were

washing clothes earlier, weren't you?"

"Oh, yes. Then hanging it, and taking it in later."

"Your families work together."

"That's the way. Elsa and I are like sisters."

"Is she the older one?"

"A couple of years."

Tommy felt a nervousness rising up, but he made himself go ahead. "How old are you, then?"

She raised her chin. "I'm sixteen." A few seconds of silence hung in the air until Anita spoke again. "Here she comes, with more wood." After another pause, she said, "Thank you for helping us."

"You're welcome." He put his hat on his head. "I guess I'd better go find a place where these horses can eat some grass."

As he turned away with the horses, he became aware that Red and Raimundo had been watching. No harm done, he figured. He hadn't done anything out of line.

Then it occurred to him that someone else might have taken in the scene as well. Looking back, he saw the dark stare of Faustino Romero. Tommy breathed in, stood up straight, and walked away with the horses.

New thoughts flooded in. If Anita was sixteen, Faustino might have been stuck on her for as much as a year or more. And he might have a motive for taking his horses out and brushing them when he did. With the families all so close, he would have an idea of when the girls would come out to wash laundry, boil corn, or do whatever work they did outside. Faustino would know when the family had killed their last pig and therefore what they had for dinner.

Privacy might be a small commodity in a group like this. And yet, Tommy had known of families with fourteen or sixteen kids, Mexican and otherwise. Some of these families lived in small houses, and Ma and Pa still found enough privacy after the first few kids to produce a few more. As he heard more than once among the bunkhouse hands, if people want to do something, they'll find a way to do it.

Tommy stopped the horses and climbed onto Pete so he could ride bareback. He was sure he was going to have to wander a ways from the village in order to find grass. He had at least another hour of daylight, and if the grazing was good, he could loiter in the light of the moon.

The sun was slipping behind the hills when Pete lifted his nose to the breeze and nickered. The other horse perked up as well.

Tommy peered to the east and saw a horse and rider poking along in his direction. He relaxed his gaze for a minute, and when the pair drew closer, he saw that it was Gabriel on the old, dull-brown horse with thin hindquarters. Tommy waited, listening to the sound of Pete and the other horse munching grass.

Gabriel was riding bareback with a hemp halter and rope that some punchers called a McCarty. He stopped the horse and slid off.

"Hey, Gabriel, did you come out to check on me?"

"No, my father sent me out to look for a burro."

"What kind? I haven't seen one."

"He's an old burro. Grey. He belongs to Milena, and he doesn't come back for two days. My father said, since you are out here, we can look for him and bring him back if we can find him."

Tommy looked at the two horses that were engrossed in cropping grass. "I guess I can," he said. "I can always stay out with these boys a little longer. We'll look for the donkey before it gets too dark." He pulled Pete around, put his hands on the horse's withers and backbone, and boosted himself onto the solid back. Gabriel swung aboard the old horse, and the party began to amble northwest.

Tommy did not bother to keep his voice low as he asked, "Do they just let these donkeys wander all over?"

"Most of the time, they use the burros for work. For sheep camps, or to carry firewood. But this one, he is old, and Milena doesn't have any sheep to take care of. Well, she has sheep, but another person in the family takes care of them. And the old burro, he doesn't go very far."

Tommy studied the landscape ahead of him. "If he came out this way, he might have ended up on Cushman's land, and they would have run him off. The animals don't know the difference, but you can see where someone plowed the section lines a few years back. Cushman always told us to run off anything that didn't belong."

Gabriel nodded, and his horse jolted along.

Dusk fell as they continued to angle northwest. The red-orange sunset faded to a pale yellow, and the rangeland was speckled with low shadows. Tommy picked out a section line and rode toward it. Out of caution he did not cross it but rode alongside of it. Gabriel caught up and fell in next to him.

"See, this is the line," said Tommy. "Cush-

71

man's pretty jealous. He told us not to step foot on his land again, and I don't want to unless it's necessary."

They were headed north now, with the sunset at their left. As they came to a low rise, Tommy saw something out of place. Up ahead and to the left where the land dipped and rose again, a small heap caught the fading light. Tommy rode ahead, keeping to the side of the line. The closer he got, the more he began to dread. Fifty yards away, he said, "That might be it."

With his heart beating stronger, he nudged his horse and crossed the section line. Gabriel rode along beside him until the old horse stopped. Pete snuffled and turned his head aside, and Red's horse milled. Tommy hung on with his legs and got the horses to stand still. He separated the ropes and slid off.

Leading the two horses, he walked forward, conscious of stepping on Cushman's land. Gabriel had slid off and was walking with him. They stopped a few yards from the dead burro.

The animal lay with its front legs crossed and its head stretched out. Its body had swollen in the summer heat, and a dark crusty stain was visible on the ribs behind the shoulder. Closer, Tommy saw where the blood had soaked into the ground below the chest.

Tommy met Gabriel's eyes in the fading light.

"He's dead," said Gabriel.

"Someone shot him. Not a hundred yards from the line. They could have chased him away, but they shot him like a dog."

CHAPTER FOUR

The old scrap lumber had a musty smell as Tommy held a piece upright and split it with a hatchet. He understood that the *gente,* or people, had hauled in several wagonloads of salvage lumber and had cut it up to make their houses, sheepherder shacks, and outbuildings. Split and broken pieces, trimmed-off ends, lumber warped beyond use, and termite-eaten pieces ended up on the woodpile. From there, Tommy was transferring it to a smaller pile of usable firewood.

From across the yard came the light, laughing voices of Anita and Elsa. Red was helping them dip the boiled corn out of the cauldron, and it sounded as if he was keeping the two girls entertained.

Off to the right and beyond the fire pit a ways, Faustino Romero sat on a chair and shined a saddle. Using a cloth that he dipped in a can of oil, he wiped the leather straps and the wooden tree. The Mexican saddle had a large, flat, wooden pommel as well as other parts of the wooden frame visible. Faustino again wore a clean set of clothes, the likes of which a merchant would wear. He also wore an ornate sombrero, black with white stitching, round with a large, upturned brim.

Close to Faustino stood his uncle Alejo, Elsa's father. Alejo was short and dark-complexioned, in contrast with his nephew, who had a light complexion and was as tall sitting down as Alejo was standing up. As they pattered along in a low conversation, Alejo kept his eye on Red. Well should he, Tommy thought. Elsa, at two years older than Anita, was almost spilling over with womanhood.

Tommy felt a mild resentment at having to work by himself, on his knees, splitting weathered lumber, while Red frolicked with the girls. On the other hand, he didn't mind being left out of the watchful stare of Alejo and Faustino.

Anita separated herself from the others and carried a pail toward the house. She was wearing a light blue dress that swished as she walked. She veered in Tommy's direction, so he stood up.

"See?" she said. "This is what it looks like when it's cooked."

The corn looked as he would have expected, swollen and dull-hued and not very interesting, but he appreciated Anita showing it to him. He thought she was sharing it with him because he had invested some work in it, what with hauling the water and coaxing the fire into flame.

A dog began barking, so Tommy moved to his left to get a better view of the yard. Coming up the slope from the creek were two riders he recognized — Fred Berwick and Walt McKinney.

Tommy stepped forward with Anita close by, and Red did the same with Elsa a couple of yards away. Faustino and Alejo came closer as well, so Fred and Walt had something of an audience.

The two riders stopped. Fred wore clean clothes as was his habit, and his light tan vest caught the sunlight. He was clean-shaven as usual. Walt, on the other hand, had a few days' worth of stubble the color of dirty straw, and his clothes looked as if he had slept in them for a while. He was wearing his six-gun today, a Colt with a small, rounded, yellowish handle sticking out in cross-draw position. He did not look at anyone in particular as he took out the makings for a cigarette.

Fred let his eyes sweep over Tommy and

Red. With a squint he said, "Good mornin', boys. Kind of surprised to see you here, but it's all the same. I've got a message from Vinch Cushman."

Red had his thumbs in his belt and his head tipped back. "Go ahead."

"Well, it's like this. Vinch is doin' what he said he would. He's brought in a crew of men with mules and scrapers, and they're cuttin' a lateral ditch. As soon as they close off the creek, the water will flow into a low spot and accumulate to make a pond." Fred paused.

"And?" said Red.

"And," Fred continued, "if anyone crosses the line to interfere, there's goin' to be trouble." His eyes settled on Tommy, and he said, "Sorry to be the one to have to carry this kind of news, but that's the way things are."

"I'm not surprised. And I don't blame you." At the edge of his vision, Tommy saw that Raimundo and Gabriel had joined the semicircle facing the visitors. Fred had his hands crossed and resting on his saddle horn. Walt had hung back, watching, and even though he had lit his cigarette, it seemed as if the two of them might leave.

Red's voice rose on the air. "Who killed the donkey?"

Fred did not flinch. He said, "I wasn't there."

Walt said nothing as he slouched in his seat. With his shifty eyes, dirty-looking stubble, drooping cigarette, and wrinkled clothes, he looked like a saddle tramp.

Red spoke again. "I think it was a cheap thing to do."

Walt sat up a little and held his cigarette between his thumb and second finger. His stubbled chin moved as he said, "You shouldn't worry about it. It's none of your business."

"I just think it was a sneaky thing to do, like some egg-suckin' dog."

Walt stiffened. He said, "You might want to watch what you say. There's more than one way to dig your grave with your mouth. Fat men eat too much, and stupid men talk too much."

"Tell that to your pal Lew Greer. They call him the fat man here."

"Why don't you tell him, the next chance you get?" Walt turned his horse and began to move away.

Keeping his voice down, Red said to Tommy, "I think he shot that donkey. And all the time I figured Greer did it."

Tommy shrugged. He was keeping an eye on the riders.

The horses sauntered away, hips shifting and tails switching. Two dogs started up and went after them, barking. They were the usual two dogs, medium-sized, mixed breed, one light and one dark. Gabriel began to take off after them, and Raimundo said something in Spanish. Gabriel stopped.

The dogs kept following and barking. The riders reached the creek and crossed over, splashing in the low water. The brown-and-black dog followed, still barking. Tommy wished the dog would turn back. Up on the other side, in a matter-of-fact but deliberate manner, Walt drew his pistol and shot the dog. It yelped once and slumped in a heap. The horses took off at a gallop.

Faustino's face went hard, and so did Raimundo's. The girls had an expression of fear and disbelief. The incident had happened so quickly, with no buildup and no trailing away, that it took a moment to sink in.

Red gave a tight, sideways scowl. "Sons of bitches," he said.

"You might have said more to them than you needed to." Tommy moistened his lips as he watched the last of the retreating horses.

Red shook his head. "They've set their minds to trouble, that's what."

Tommy went back to splitting wood as Anita carried the pail into the house. Red walked with Elsa to resume ladling out the corn, but the merry laughter was all gone. Gabriel crossed the creek to bring back the dead dog. Raimundo, Alejo, and Faustino stayed in a close group and talked things over in Spanish.

The stack of kindling grew, with the pale yellow of the interior of the old pine lumber contrasting with the weathered grey exterior. Tommy stayed focused on keeping his fingers and thumb clear of the hatchet head. Once in a while he looked up and around. Both of the girls had gone inside, and Red was busying himself with the horses. The men continued talking.

Gabriel stopped to visit, his shoes and lower pant legs wet from crossing the creek.

"I'm sorry about what happened," Tommy said.

"There's not much we can do."

"Walt didn't have to do what he did." Tommy motioned with his head. "It looks like the men have plenty to talk about."

"That's Faustino. When something happens, he wants everyone to listen to him."

"Is he some kind of a leader in your group? I thought your father was."

"My father is older, and he knows many

things, so people listen to him. But Faustino is important, too. He is like a mayor. He helps manage all the papers, and he helps with the money."

"You mean he lends money?"

"Sometimes he does that, too. But he collects money, to pay the taxes and to buy the things we need."

"Oh, I see. He makes trips to buy supplies, like flour and beans and rice."

"Yes, and for other things." Gabriel pointed at the pile of scrap lumber. "He bought all the wood."

"Ah-hah. So he's kind of a banker, and kind of a business manager."

"That's it."

"He looks as if he's a little better off than some of the others. Got more money. Better-lookin' horses. I guess that comes from not being married yet."

Gabriel laughed. "My father says that the people with money always have money, and poor people are always poor."

"I've heard that, too, and from the little I've seen, it seems to be true. My uncle's that way. Says he was born poor and he'll die poor. Maybe he will. Did Faustino come from a family with a little more money?"

"A little. From his father's side."

"Now, he's kind of a cousin of yours, isn't he?"

"Yes. His mother is sister to my uncle Alejo. They are short and dark. His father, Don Patricio, was taller and not so dark. He said his family was from Spain. So he was always a little better. He had a hotel in Alamogordo. But he had bad drinking, and he lost too much money on horse races. One day he drank a glass of brandy, and he died. They say someone put something in his drink, to stop his heart just like that. Nobody knows for sure. But my father says that is the way life is. We never know the hour when death can come."

Tommy frowned. "So the two sons came here to try to make a better life? There's not much money in homesteading."

"They go with the family. Everything was finished in Alamogordo."

"That's too bad. Their mother, too?"

"Yes, and their father did not have much by the time he died. My father says all Don Patricio had left was his pride and a few *duros* and *pesetas*."

"What are those?"

"Spanish coins."

The voices of the three men rose on the air and went silent. As the men dispersed, Faustino picked up his saddle stand and carried it with the saddle to his house. Raimundo beckoned to his son, so Gabriel said goodbye to Tommy and took off to join his father.

Tommy resumed splitting wood, and within a couple of minutes he heard footsteps and the jingle of spurs. He turned and stood up as Red drew nearer.

Red had a stem of grass in his mouth. He shifted it from one side to another and said, "I think they've been talkin' about us."

"They're probably talking about the whole mess, and we're part of it."

"I get the feeling that those other two don't care for us. You'd think they'd be glad to have us. I don't know how much these Mexicans are for puttin' up a fight."

"It doesn't seem to me that they want to fight. They'd rather avoid it."

Red gave a slow shake of the head. "If it was my donkey or my dog, I think I'd do something about it."

"They're not in a good spot. Both those animals crossed the line. I know animals cross both ways all the time and don't know any better, but Vinch's men have some justification. It's not right, but they've got a leg to stand on."

"Well, I thought Walt was all right at one time, but I've changed my mind."

"I can't say that I ever liked him, but I sure don't care for him now." Tommy's gaze traveled to the Villarreal house. He imagined Anita inside, amassing the ground corn as Gabriel turned the handle on the grinder. "I don't know how much good we're doing here," he said.

"Oh, we can give it a little while. If they want us gone, we'll be able to tell. But like I said before, they ought to be glad we're here."

"Maybe so, but I'd just as soon not wear out our welcome. I think I'll take the horses out to graze and make myself scarce for a while."

"Do you want me to go with you?"

"No, it's something I can do by myself. And I don't mind being alone."

The shadows of evening were beginning to soften when Tommy led the two horses back into the village. He was tired and hungry, on edge and worried. He thought he would feel much better with a plate of food and the presence of Anita, but he didn't know what to expect.

He found Red lounging against the saddles in the lean-to.

"About time you got back. I spent just about the whole day here by myself."

"No girls to keep you company?"

"Seems like they're keepin' 'em inside."

"Huh. Well, I'm going to water these horses. Did you eat?"

"Oh, yeah. Gabriel brought me some food on a plate."

The thought of actual food made Tommy's stomach feel even emptier. As he led the horses to the trough and let them drink, he made himself be patient. If no one brought him food, he would have to get by.

Back at the lean-to, he moped for a few minutes until Gabriel appeared with a lantern and a tan crockery plate of food. The sight of the food restored Tommy's faith in the Mexicans' sense of hospitality, and the aroma raised his spirits right away. Half of the plate was covered with beans, and the other half had a soft-looking meat soaking in a red sauce. Gabriel handed him the plate and hung the lantern on a nail overhead. Tommy sat down on a saddle and dug in as Gabriel crouched on his heels and hugged his knees.

"This is unbelievable. It tastes so good that I want to eat it all at once. I was starving." He took another spoonful. "What is it?"

"*Chicharrones.* The skin of the pig."

"Oh, cracklin's. Fried pork rinds."

"That's right. Then they cook it in the red chile."

"I can't believe how good it is. Perfect combination with the beans."

"The last of the pig. We kill it about a week ago, and we fry the skin then."

Tommy recalled that he had eaten pork each day with these people. "Does your family eat a whole pig in a week?"

"Oh, no. Each house takes a share. Next time, maybe someone kills a sheep, and everyone takes some."

"That makes sense." Tommy pointed his spoon at the fire pit, where Alejo was leaning over and laying some of the split kindling in place for a fire. "Is someone going to cook something?"

"Not right now. I think Faustino wants to speak."

"Oh." Tommy noticed that the tripod had been taken away. Alejo crouched and struck a match, and a small flame grew at the edge of the crisscrossed kindling. The light reflected on the man's dark features, and for a moment, Tommy imagined being in another time and place. In his fancy, he was a captive among the Apaches.

Gabriel's voice brought him back. "There's Faustino now."

Alejo was still crouched, fanning with his

86

hat, as Faustino came into view and stood by the fire. The flame brightened, casting a glow on the white embroidery of his black jacket and hat. On second glance, Tommy saw that the man wore a gunbelt with inlaid black holsters and white-handled pistols. To all appearances, he had dressed for his speech.

Tommy finished his meal and held his plate forward. "Thanks, Gabriel. That was wonderful. Please tell your mother."

"Do you want more?"

"Oh, no, thanks." Tommy was disappointed with himself for turning down the offer, but he wanted to be polite, and he imagined the family wanted to hear what Faustino had to say.

Gabriel took the plate. "I'll be right back."

Tommy watched the plate go away. He could have eaten two more servings of that delicious food, but he told himself to be satisfied with what he had. He turned to Red and said, "Do you know anything about the speech coming up?"

Red shook his head. "News to me."

Alejo stood up and chatted with Faustino as a couple of other men joined the group. Raimundo came out of the house and headed for the gathering. Gabriel hurried over to the lean-to and motioned to Red and Tommy.

"Come on. He's going to talk now."

Tommy said, "Do they want us to listen?"

"Oh, yes. It's important." Gabriel stood on his tiptoes and blew out the lantern.

By the time they reached the area lit by the fire, another man had arrived. Tommy counted them. Raimundo, Alejo, Faustino, a man who could only be Faustino's brother, and two men Tommy had not seen before. With eight households in total and one of them belonging to a widow, that left one man missing. Tommy figured he was out tending to sheep. Another boy about Gabriel's age showed up and stood behind one of the men Tommy did not know. Ten altogether, all men and boys.

Faustino began his speech in Spanish, with what seemed like a set of preliminary expressions of courtesy. Then, to Tommy's surprise, he switched to English.

"Here is the problem we have today. In the first place, the big rancher Cooshmon does not like us. That is nothing new. Always there is someone who does not like Mexican people, and this one he is jealous because he wants all the pasture. *Bien.* And now he wants us to leave. I say, why? We have been here two years, and now he wants us to leave? Is it for the grass? Or is it because we have sheep? Or is it because we are Mexicans?" Faustino held out his hands, palms up.

He went on. "Maybe it is all of these things. He is jealous. He is full of hate. He wants to take our water so that we should go." Faustino paused and waved his arm. "But nobody wants to go. We are all stubborn. *Muy tercos. ¿No es cierto?*"

A rumble of agreement went around the group, followed by comments. Tommy caught words he knew — *casa, borrego, tierra.* House, sheep, land. He heard the word *zopilote.* That was the new one — buzzard. Then he heard a word, quite clear, that he didn't know. *Alacrán.*

He turned to Gabriel. "What does that mean, *alacrán?*"

Gabriel cupped his hand, held it downward, and moved his fingers. "Big spider."

Faustino cleared his throat, then again, louder. When he had the floor, he said, "But I think we should go. Leave before he does any more damage, before he hurts anyone. We come back with the law."

"No, no, no," ran the voices. Tommy picked out another word several times — *aquí.* Here. The people wanted to stay here.

"Very well," said Faustino. "We know he wants us to leave. But I ask, why now? Why, after two years?"

No one came forth with an answer.

"Well, here is what happens. Here come these two boys, young Americans. I want to say Yankees, but maybe they are from Texas. I do not know. But they work for Cooshmon, and he does not like them. I do not know why. But he runs them away. They come here. Then Cooshmon kills a burro and a dog, and he wants to cut our water."

Tommy felt all the eyes of the group as they stared at him and Red. He did not agree with Faustino's version of the cause or even of the order of the events, but he did not know if he had a voice in the argument.

Faustino put the heels of his hands on the jutting white handles of his six-guns. Raising his head so that the firelight caught his face and the underside of the brim of his sombrero, he said, "I am not afraid to stay and fight. Neither is my brother."

All eyes turned to the brother, who stood with his arms across his chest and his fists pushing out his biceps.

Faustino held his hands at chest level, turned outward a little. "We have choices. We can leave and come back later. We can stay and fight Cooshmon, who is angry with these boys. Or we can stay, let the boys go, and see if Cooshmon still gives us trouble. I do not decide, because I am one and you are many. But I will say this. I am not afraid."

Alejo stepped forward and spoke. *"Que se vayan."*

No one looked at Tommy and Red. The men all seemed to be making an effort to look at nothing in particular. Tommy turned to Gabriel and asked, "What did he say?"

"That you should leave."

Red said, in a low voice, "I wonder what the rest of 'em think."

Tommy felt a chill. He drew his elbows against his ribs to try to keep steady. In answer to Red, he said, "No one else is saying anything different." He let his eyes wander over the group. Raimundo did not avoid him, so Tommy spoke to the man who had been their host. "It's not necessary to take a vote. We'll go. Or at least I'll go. Red can decide for himself."

"I won't stay where I'm not wanted."

As the two boys turned and headed toward the lean-to and their horses, Raimundo said, "You don't have to leave tonight."

"It's just as well," said Tommy. "Let your people be at peace."

"This gives me pain," said Raimundo. "I would not turn you from my house."

"I don't see it that way. You don't need to apologize."

Raimundo seemed relieved. "You are good boys. You show good understanding."

"Thanks. We don't have any hard feelings." Tommy gave him a nod of assurance and continued on his way to the lean-to.

Gabriel lit the lantern again to show light for the boys as they packed their gear. The group of men around the fire broke up, and the fire died down. Alejo had not been prodigal with the wood to begin with, and the split pine lumber burned fast. The night drew into just the lantern, the boys, and the horses.

Tommy pulled the leather strings tight to hold down his bedroll and war bag. He led Pete out a few steps and snugged the front cinch. Gabriel was still holding the lantern for Red, so Tommy stood alone with his horse between him and the light.

A faint rustle caused him to turn to his left. In the semidarkness he saw the form of a young woman.

He spoke in a low voice. "Hello, there."

Anita's voice was soft and lovely to his ears. "I came to say goodbye."

"That's very nice of you."

"I brought this for your horse." She held

up her hand, and he saw that she had a corn tortilla.

He took it and said, "Thanks." He held it under Pete's nose, and within a few seconds the horse had curled his lip and taken in the delicacy.

Anita's voice was soft as she said, "He likes it."

"Yes, he does." Tommy met her eyes in the imperfect light. "I hope I can see you again. I hope this isn't *adios.*"

She smiled and said, "No, just *hasta luego.*"

"I don't think your father is angry with me."

"Oh, no. He knows that you are going away so that there will be peace here. Time passes. Things change."

"I hope so." He held out his hand, and her fingers touched his.

She faded back into the night as Gabriel came forward with the lantern. He led the way through the yard as Tommy and Red followed with their horses. Raimundo appeared as they rounded the front corner of the Villarreal house. Alejo and Faustino stood a couple of yards back.

Both Tommy and Red had taken their gunbelts out of their saddlebags and had buckled them on. With his pistol on his hip and his rifle in the scabbard, Tommy felt equipped and capable. He could see that Alejo and Faustino were looking over the horses, rifles, and six-guns.

Raimundo stepped forward and shook hands with both of them. "You will come again to my house," he said. "You are always welcome."

"Thank you," said Tommy. "And thank you for everything while we were here."

Red's voice was forceful. "Thanks from me, too. We'll be back."

Tommy led his horse out a few steps and turned him. He set his reins, grabbed a hank of mane, and held the saddle horn to pull himself aboard. He settled in and said, "So long, Gabriel."

Red swung up into the saddle, pulled on the reins to make his horse tuck his head, and backed up a couple of steps. He looked around as if to find a face at the edge of the light, then tipped his hat and said goodbye to Gabriel. He touched his spurs to his horse, and the two riders moved out of the lamplight.

A hundred yards from the houses, as they rode into the night, Red spoke. "That was quite a speech he worked up."

"I think he's used to it."

"Seemed to me he had things out of kilter,

but I didn't see a way around it. He was determined to get rid of us."

"Sure seemed that way."

Red sounded a bit haughty as he said, "Don't know how good a judgment it was. We could have been of help to them."

"Maybe he didn't think they needed our help."

"Puh. It was because of you, you know. He's got eyes for that girl, and he didn't like you gettin' in the way."

Tommy held his tongue. Maybe Red was just getting even for Tommy saying he had provoked Walt McKinney. None of it mattered much, once things had taken their course. And besides, Anita had come out to say goodbye. That was something to keep to himself and appreciate.

CHAPTER FIVE

Red was sitting on his bedroll and smoking a cigarette when Tommy woke up. The horses were making a commotion, shuffling their feet and breathing hard.

Tommy rose up on one elbow. The world filled in around him. To the east, sunlight was breaking through a thin wall of clouds. The Mexican village was about a mile west. He and Red had come this far in the night, downstream, until they found bushes tall enough to tie the horses. The creek did not make any sound, not like the stream on the Muleshoe that splashed and burbled over rocks.

He had thought of the Muleshoe before he went to sleep. Here on the dry, almost treeless plains, he recalled a night in late winter when the full moon shed its light on a heavy blanket of snow that lay on the pines and cedars. He had thought of that scene many times. Life at the Muleshoe had been cold and windy, and when the weak sunlight of spring began to melt the ice, the mud took over. But he remembered the good parts, like that one pretty night, the gurgling stream, the deer and elk, the blue grouse, and the snowshoe hares. It seemed like a world away, that time before Vinch Cushman or Red Armstrong, but it was less than six months ago. He left because he was making half a man's wages. Now he was making nothing.

"What's wrong with the horses?" he asked.

"Nothin'. They're just restless. One moves, and then the other does. They need to be used more."

"Maybe they're hungry." Tommy sat up and flipped the blankets aside.

"They ate all day yesterday. They could do with a ride."

"What do you have in mind?"

Red blew out a stream of smoke. "We could go to town."

"To town? What for? We were just there a couple of days ago."

"I'd like to know what Vinch is up to, if he's really bringin' in a grading crew."

"I would guess he is, or already has. Fred said he had already started."

Red spit away a fleck of tobacco. "He says what he's told to say. And besides, we need some grub."

"We still have what we bought." Tommy reached for his boots.

"Just a couple of cans."

Tommy pulled on his boots and stood up. "Why don't we do it this way? Rather than load up everything, we can leave the camp as it is. I'll stay here. You can do what you want to do, and I'll mind the camp and keep to myself."

Red took a long drag on his cigarette. "I guess I could. You don't seem to be in a very good mood."

"Oh, I'm all right. Sometimes it just feels like I got filled up on things. Maybe a day on my own will help me empty out."

Red lifted his head and looked across the creek to the north. "This should be a good place for it."

Tommy set his hat forward to block out the glare of the sun. Up on the rangeland away from the creek, heat rose from the ground at the same time that it poured down from above. Now in late morning, the air did not stir. The only sounds came from the shift of Pete's hooves, the drag of the lead rope, and the grazing of the horse as he tore and munched the dry grass.

Small black ants and larger red ones went

about their work in the bare earth between the clumps of curled grass. So did the dry-backed grey beetles and the smaller black ones. Somewhere out there, Tommy knew, there were sparrows and larks and black-birds that would eat these bugs and others. Maybe the birds were shaded up right now, like the rabbits. He looked up and saw a lone hawk floating in the sky.

The world seemed to stretch away forever in all directions, though he knew that the Mexican village lay to the west, and beyond that, the White Wings Ranch had its building and corrals. To the south and west lay Fenton, where Red would be satisfying his curiosity or at least his restlessness to be doing something and going somewhere.

Tommy glanced over his shoulder toward camp. He had wandered quite a ways as he let his horse graze. For as much as he liked being alone out under the open sky, he felt an uneasiness, a sense of having left his rifle, his pistol, and his saddle next to a bush in full view, almost a mile away. He should go back.

He gave a tug on the lead rope. Pete raised his head, turned, and fell into line. Tommy struck a course across the prairie, keeping an eye out for snakes as always. A greyish-brown bird, smaller than a meadowlark, rose up from the sagebrush and flitted away. Tommy stepped aside to avoid a gopher hole and looked back to see that Pete did the same.

As the land sloped down toward the creek, he saw the tops of the chokecherry bushes where he and Red had tied the horses. He was a hundred yards downstream, where the creek spread out and made a mudhole. He smelled the stale water and saw a cloud of gnats hovering at eye level. He turned left to go downstream a ways further before he would cross.

The creek took a turn between two low ledges of pale clay. Beyond the gap, the area widened out into a green, grassy area. Tommy was about to take a peek when he saw the tan hip and white rump of an antelope.

He sank back and took the slack out of the lead rope, then turned and retraced the way he had come. He passed the muddy area on his left and continued upstream until he reached a dry spot across from the camp. The water was about a foot wide and three inches deep at this point, so he jumped across. Pete jumped as well and settled with a heave of breath.

Tommy felt jittery as he tied the horse to a bush, then leaned over the saddle on the ground and drew the rifle out of its scabbard. The antelope might not stay long. This was the time they would come for a drink of water before they laid up in the middle part of the day. He took a deep breath to steady himself. He might get one shot at best.

He did not know what the approach was like from this side of the creek, so he decided to go back to the spot where he had gotten as close as he did.

Within a few minutes he was crouched at the low ledge where the water flowed. He did not dare walk around through the gap. He ran too great a chance of spooking the antelope — if they were still there. He was going to have to crawl. And so he did.

Crawling on all fours was hard enough, but carrying the rifle and making sure he didn't poke it into the dirt called for an awkward, hobbling motion. He worked his way up the slope, and once on top, he had to keep crawling until the creek bottom came into view. As it did, he crouched lower and lower, hoping to see the animals before they saw him.

A spot of color caused him to sink back and take off his hat. Rising a quarter of an inch at a time, he moved forward. He expected to see a group of three or four, which was what he had been seeing at this time of year. He would have to place them, take a cautious look, and decide on his best chance. As he worked his way up, however, none came into view. Then he located the one he had seen before, or at least he assumed it was the same one. It was turned so that the sun did not shine so bright on it. The animal's head was lowered in a grazing posture. Tommy waited. At last the antelope raised its head and showed a small set of dark horns. A young buck.

Tommy got set, checking for cactus before he settled into a prone position. He guessed the animal to be about a hundred yards away, not a long shot for an antelope but still a small target, turned as it was at a three-quarter angle. Tommy levered in a shell and got situated again. He put the bead of his front sight behind the animal's shoulder, squirmed to line up the rear sight, and pulled the trigger.

The rifle stock slapped him on the cheekbone as the antelope lurched. It ran straight ahead about twenty yards, stopped, hunched up, and spilled over.

Tommy felt a great release of tension, but he waited to make sure the animal did not get up. A hind leg was kicking, and then it went still.

A flash of color to the lower left of his vision caused him to look in that direction. Two more antelope, a doe and a fawn, were racing up out of the creek bed and straight away from him. Tommy watched them run. They had been right under his nose, out of view because of the contour of the ground.

Back to his own antelope, he saw that it had not moved. Its white underside and rump stood out against the pale, dry grass where it had fallen. Tommy stood up, walked down the slope, jumped over the water, and crossed the green creek bottom. Up on the other side, he paused to gather his thoughts.

He had killed his first antelope, and now he had to clean it. He was glad not to have Red or someone else telling him what to do, but he needed to get started and not fuss around. He knew that much. A hunter needed to clean his antelope right away, especially in hot weather. With the kind of hair antelope had, great insulation for cold weather, the meat spoiled fast.

Tommy laid his rifle on a low growth of sagebrush so that it did not touch the ground, and he took out his pocketknife. He told himself to be careful. Keep the knife pointed away. Don't hurry. He had gutted and skinned a couple of deer. This should not be all that different, except that he didn't have a tree to hang it from. He would have to skin it on the ground.

He cut off all four lower legs and began to cut the hide along the inside of the hind legs. He thought he would do a cleaner job if he skinned it first and then gutted it. At least that was the way it worked with deer when he hung them. As he continued to cut the hide along the belly and up to the chest, though, he began to wonder. The thick, white, hollow lengths of hair flew everywhere and stuck on his bloody hands. Now he began to feel awkward, cutting from one angle and then another as he tried to separate the hide from the carcass. Hair scattered like chicken feathers.

A voice from behind him made him jump, and the knife jerked in his hand.

"Got a good one, did you?"

Tommy swallowed as he raised up and looked around. On the slope behind him to the east, a man in a drover's coat sat atop a flecked grey horse with dark ears.

"Bill Lockwood," said the man. "I think we've met."

"I believe so," said Tommy. "You took me by surprise there."

"Sorry if I spooked you. I heard a shot, so I came over to see what was goin' on. I saw two other antelope runnin' away, so I had an idea."

"Well, that's what it is. I don't think it should bother anyone,"

"Oh, no. Not at all. I can even give you a hand if you like."

"I can do it myself."

"I'm sure you can. But it goes easier if someone holds a leg for you and keeps the animal from floppin' one way or another."

Tommy did not like the idea of someone watching his uncertain moves, but he knew the man was right. "I guess," he said.

"Good enough." Lockwood turned his horse and dismounted. He took off his gloves, put them in his saddlebag, and led the grey horse forward. "Let's see where you are. Uh-huh. Let me hold this front leg, and I'll stay out of your way. Oh, and just a suggestion. If you cut from the inside out, you'll get less hair. The more of it you can keep off the meat, the better it'll be. You'll still get some, of course, but you want to pick off as much as you can."

Tommy bent over and went to work. The white hair continued to fly. It stuck on his knife and on his hands. He felt so inept in front of Lockwood that he began to wish he hadn't shot the antelope. A white hair stuck on the tip of his nose, and he blew it away in exasperation.

"You're doin' fine," said Lockwood. "Once you get him opened up, just keep the hide rolled back, and you'll get a lot less of this."

Tommy worked on with his knife, trimming the skin from the carcass. The antelope had very little fat, and the hide was easy to nick, but before long he had one side skinned. Lockwood, still holding his reins, moved around to the other side and held the hind leg. Tommy rested his back for a minute and resumed his work.

When he had the whole body skinned, he cut through the neck muscle and found a joint between two vertebrae.

"This part is hard," said Lockwood, "But it can be done. Just don't break your knife. When you get partway through, we can try to twist it."

When they had that much done, Tommy stood up to catch his breath. The sun had moved overhead. He figured he had been at this work for an hour already.

Lockwood said, "I think it would be a good idea to pick off all the hair you can before you spill out the guts and blood."

Tommy took another deep breath and nodded. The outside of the animal was starting to dry, and the abdomen was swelling. He worked as fast as he could.

Then came the time to open the cavity and empty it. Tommy rolled up his sleeves and plunged in. His arms were stained red almost to the elbows when he was finished, and a strong, gamy smell rose to his nostrils.

"Well, that's got it," said Lockwood. "You're lucky about one thing. It's not very often you kill an antelope near water. I'll wait here if you want to go clean up."

Tommy washed up as well as he could and splashed his face while he was at it, but he was still tired and sweaty when he returned to the site of the kill. Lockwood, meanwhile, did not have a speck of blood on him, and even though he had been wearing the duster all this time, he had not broken a sweat.

"I'll tell you what," he said. "We can put this carcass on my horse, and he'll carry it to your camp."

"Well, thanks. I'm camped back this way."

"I think I saw it. That is, I assume it's your horse that's standing with his nose in the bush and his tail swishin' flies."

Tommy paused. The man didn't miss much, but if he was up to any trouble, he would have done something by now. "All right," he said. "How shall we go about it?"

"Let's try this. Cut a slit between these two ribs, and we can slip that over the saddle horn. You can walk alongside and hold him in place. This short a distance, I think we can get by without tyin' him to the D-rings."

Red showed up in camp in the late afternoon. He had a cut across his cheek, and his blue eyes were glazed and bloodshot. Tommy did not catch a whiff of whiskey, but he guessed Red had been drinking.

"How did you cut your cheek?"

Red spoke as he dismounted with his back turned. "Low branch on a tree."

Tommy wondered where he would have found a tree tall enough to have a low branch that high. "What's new in town?"

"Didn't spend much time there. You killed an antelope, huh?"

"How did you know that?"

"I saw Bill Lockwood. Too bad you didn't get a deer. The meat's better. This thing'll spoil before we eat very much of it."

"We'll eat good while it lasts."

"I imagine. Let me water my horse." Red pulled his reins through his hand and made the ends flick.

"I'll start a fire. I gathered some dead sagebrush."

Tommy had a blaze going, with puffs and wisps of pungent smoke drifting up, when Red came back to the campsite.

"What all did you get in town?"

"Nothin'."

Tommy took a breath to keep from saying anything.

"Talked to Fred."

"Oh. What did he have to say?"

"Vinch hired two men to take our place. Look more like gunhands than cowpunchers."

"Is that what Fred told you?"

"I seen 'em."

"In town?"

"No. Out on the job. They're watchin' over the project."

"Where were you?"

"On the line. Me on one side, Fred on the other. Two men with scrapers makin' a reservoir to hold the water when they get ready to dam the creek. And these two hired hands lookin' like a couple of bulldogs."

"When do you think they'll cut off the water?"

"Tomorrow or the next day. They're pilin' the dirt, and then they have to push it in just right. It won't take that much to close it. They just need a place for the water to back up, and a neck they can plug."

"It makes you wonder why someone wants to go to that much trouble to make things hard on other people."

Red poked at the dirt with his bootheel. "I'll tell you what it makes me want to do. Makes me want to blow it up."

Tommy had an image of an earthen mound exploding into a spray of dirt and water. It seemed like a flamboyant idea on Red's part, but Tommy kept his comments to himself as he laid a twisted branch of sagebrush on the fire.

"Don't think I don't know how."

"I didn't say anything."

"At first I thought it would do to just go up there at night and cut a hole in the bank and let the water flow through. But now I've got a mind to blow it up."

Tommy wondered if the whiskey was talking. "What changed your mind?"

"Lew Greer."

"Oh. Did you see him, too?"

"I guess I did. He came up to where I was talkin' to Fred. He told Fred to leave, and then he told me to go on my way. I told him he'd have to make me go, and he spurred his horse right over the section line and slapped me with his quirt. I'll tell you, he's not goin' to do anything like that again."

Tommy recalled having heard something similar before. He said, "I'd like to get started cooking some of that meat. We can cut out a chunk of backstrap, lay it on these rocks, and push the coals up next to it. Cook one side at a time."

"You don't think I mean it."

"I didn't say that at all. I just want to cook this meat while we've got the fire."

"Well, I know where to get what I need. Blow their dirt pile sky high."

"I've got the antelope on the other side of these bushes here. I put it in what shade there was. If you hold it, I'll cut out a good piece."

Closer now, as Red knelt to hold the carcass, Tommy caught the smell of whiskey. He leaned over the animal, cut across the grain of the meat, and began to trim it lengthwise away from the backbone.

Red went on. "These same fellas we sold the heifer to. They've got everything from dynamite to morphine."

Tommy recalled the scene that came to him every so often as a memory he wished he could forget. Six or eight men hung around, some standing and some leaning, one sitting on a stack of railroad ties. Pick-and-shovel workers, grimy section hands, a couple of loafers who looked as if they didn't get dirty very often — they had all given a casual glance at the reddish-brown, unbranded heifer and the two boys who had

111

brought it. Everyone knew what kind of a transaction it was, and no one seemed to care. A burly man in a round hat and railroader's overalls said something as he gave Red the money. Red threw back his head and laughed as he slipped the coins into his pocket. The incident had seemed like a normal moment at a railroad camp — as normal as a whiskey peddler or a whoremaster tying open the flap on his tent.

Tommy pulled the meat away from the backbone and cut deeper. "Are you thinking of going there?"

"Oh, yeah. I'd like to go tonight."

"You can't be serious."

"Why not?"

"It's dark. You don't know the country that well, once you get out a few miles. Anything could happen. It's a good fifteen miles or more."

"Nothin' to it. I'll take my bedroll and sleep out if I have to."

"Red, you ought to take a little time and think this over."

"You mean sober up. Well, I am sober. And someone's gonna be in for a surprise."

"You'd better get some food in you, anyway." Tommy lifted the strip of meat from the carcass. "Let's have a can of tomatoes each while we let this cook."

"You can go along, too, you know."

"I'd rather not. I'll hold down camp. I don't think it's a good idea, anyway." Tommy laid the antelope loin on the rocks he had put in place. The meat was about two inches thick and a foot long.

"I doubted that you'd want to go."

"What I mean is, I don't think you should go. Too many things could go wrong." Tommy took a stick and began scooting the coals toward the meat.

Red moved his bedroll near the fire and sat on it. "Well, look here, little buddy. Lots of things can go wrong. For one thing, Lew Greer runs us off of our job. Then that windbag runs us out of the Mexican camp, just when we're startin' to get somewhere with those girls. The way I see it, you can let people shove you around all your life, or you can do something about it. Just one little trick and Fat Man Greer and Big Buzzard Cushman will be eatin' crow. And when the Mexicans get their water back, that monkey-face won't have a thing to say."

Tommy figured Red must have killed the bottle just before he got to camp. The whiskey was flowing in his veins pretty well. "What do you think of Bill Lockwood?" Tommy asked.

"Oh, he's all right. Bought me a drink."

"Was that after your run-in with Lew?" Dusk was falling, and the cut on Red's cheek lay in shadow.

"Oh, yeah. But you know Lockwood. Acts like he doesn't notice a thing."

Tommy woke up at the first grey of morning. Pete had been snuffling and moving around. Tommy smelled dust on the cool air. He huddled into his blankets, thinking of the sequence he would go through as soon as he got up. Boots, jacket, hat. Take Pete to the water. Get a fire going and cook some of the meat.

He tried to imagine where Red was at the moment. He wondered if Red had made it to the railroad camp or had slept out somewhere along the way. The whole plan came back to him as a bad idea. But Red had a streak in him that didn't go along with good judgment — or, really, with doing things right. Tommy hoped Red had slept off some of his notions. Failing that, maybe the railroaders would laugh at him, ask him what the hell made him think he could buy dynamite.

Back to the moment, Tommy realized that the creek might run dry at some time today, so he had better water his horse while he could. He turned over, flipped the blankets aside, and started his day.

The sun had climbed to midmorning, and the day was warming up. What little moisture had hung in the air at sunrise was gone now. Shade was scarce. Tommy's stomach made churning sounds as it worked on the pound or so of meat he had eaten for breakfast. He had a can of peaches left, and he was going to save that delicacy for as long as he could.

He took Pete to water again. The creek was still flowing. He thought he should take Pete out to graze, but Red had said he would be back by midmorning at the latest, and Tommy did not want to go out wandering until his friend arrived.

Time passed. The shadows grew shorter at midday, and Red still did not show. The worry in Tommy's stomach began to grow. If Red slept out, he might be at the railroad camp right now. Or he could be anywhere in between.

The shadows had begun to creep out on the east side of the chokecherry bushes. Tommy sat with his eyes closed, wondering how long he would wait until he decided to do something else. Until this evening? Until the water went dry? At some point something should happen, but he didn't know what or when.

His head dipped forward, and he woke up. Pete was shifting his hooves and finishing a low nicker. Tommy stood up and walked around the bush, into the sunlight.

A rider was approaching. It was not Red. The man wore a dark hat and was riding a grey horse. Bill Lockwood.

As the man drew closer, he looked smaller than before. He was not wearing the brown dustcoat. He drew rein a few yards out from camp.

"Come on in," said Tommy.

Lockwood rode forward and dismounted. He was lean, not very tall but solid-looking. His black hat was dusty as before, and grey showed at his temples. His bushy mustache was set firm, and his coffee-colored eyes held steady.

"Good afternoon," he said.

"Good afternoon."

"You might wonder what brings me out this way again."

Tommy's eyes took in the man's gloved hands, then his gunbelt. He thought again that Lockwood might be a range detective, but he said, "I have no idea."

"Well, I'm sorry to say it, but I'm the bearer of bad news."

116

Tommy's pulse jumped. "What kind?"

Lockwood's eyes did not waver. "I'm afraid your friend Red Armstrong cashed in his chips."

A jolt hit Tommy in the pit of his stomach. His head went dizzy, and he heard himself say, "When did that happen?"

"Last night. Seems he was prowlin' around that ditch project of Vinch Cushman's. I guess Cushman expected trouble, because he had a night guard posted."

"And Red got shot?"

"That's right."

Tommy's mouth was dry, and his breath was gone. "He told me he was going up north a ways and would be back today."

"Well, he must have stopped there on his way. I'm sorry."

"It doesn't make sense."

"No, it doesn't. He was in a place where he shouldn't have been."

Tommy felt as if all of his strength had run out. He cast his eyes around at the ground in front of him. "I don't know what to say. It just doesn't —"

"I know. I hate to be the one to have to tell you."

"Someone had to, I guess. If anyone knew, or anyone cared."

"That's just it. I didn't think this was any

place for you to be, all on your own."

Tommy's eyes were swelling, and his throat was closing. "I can take care of myself."

"Maybe you can," said Lockwood. "But you can come along with me if you want. You can stay at my place until you've got a better idea."

CHAPTER SIX

Tommy looked back once as he and Lockwood rode away from the campsite. With no trees, just the chokecherry bushes where he and Red had tied their horses and the willow bush that had given a bit of shade, it didn't look like much of a camp. Even the fire pit was unnoticeable from a distance of fifty yards. Tommy wondered if that was the way his life was going to be, just stops and stays along the way and leaving hardly a mark. What was it that Gabriel had repeated from his father? Something to the effect that a person never knew the hour when death would come. That seemed to be the case with Red — eighteen years old and gone out of this world already. Tommy fought the tightness in his throat and tried to brush the thoughts away. He touched a spur to Pete and took off at a trot to catch up with Lockwood.

The grey horse was moving along at no

great hurry. Lockwood swayed in the saddle with the antelope wrapped up in Tommy's ground sheet and tied on behind.

As Tommy rode alongside, he said, "I've been thinkin' about it."

Lockwood gave a casual, rolling motion with his head. "Yeah?"

"That meat is not going to last long in this weather."

"Good chance you're right about that."

"I think I'd like to give most of it to some friends over this way. The Mexican people. We stayed with them for a little while, and this would be a way of, well, not really paying them back, but sort of returning the favor."

"Reasonable enough."

"Do you know them?"

"I've met a couple of 'em. I stopped in one day. They're friendly — to me, at least. I always get along well with Mexicans, anyway."

"If you don't mind, then, we could drop in on them."

"Sure. No trouble at all."

They rode on without talking. The horse hooves struck the ground in dull thuds, and dust rose in the warm air. Saddle leather creaked. Now and again a grasshopper whirred away with a light clacking sound and a show of pale yellow wings.

Lockwood led the way, keeping to the south side of the creek until the small group of buildings came into view. He turned the horse and rode to the water's edge, where he stopped. The grey horse lowered its muzzle to the shallow stream. Tommy let Pete stop and do the same. The water ran clear and smooth, with a few pebbles in the silty streambed. One of Pete's hooves nudged forward and roiled up a small cloud of mud.

"Water's still runnin'," said Lockwood. "I wonder how much longer it'll last."

Tommy gathered that Cushman's plans were well known. He said, "It seems to me like a lot of trouble to go to."

"That's exactly what it is. A lot of trouble."

"Does he even have a right to dam up a stream?"

"Not really. But it'll take a while to get someone to come here and do something about it. It could even go to court. Either way, by the time it's all done with, the most he'll probably have to do is let the water flow again."

From the tone of Lockwood's voice, Tommy did not think that the man sided with Cushman or even sympathized with large landowners. As far as Tommy knew, range detectives worked for cattlemen and operated under the philosophy that might made right. Lockwood was seeming less like that kind of an individual, but if he was something else, Tommy was yet to figure out what it was. With his riding gloves and his snug-fitting gunbelt, he did not look like a drover or a cowpuncher, much less a punkin-roller. He had the look of a man who spent most of his time outdoors, a little rugged to be a horse trader and certainly not slick enough to be a card sharp or a liniment salesman. Tommy wondered if he would know the man long enough to find out.

Lockwood tightened his reins, raising the horse's head, and gigged the animal into motion again. Tommy followed on Pete, crossing the creek and jogging up the slope toward the village.

The light-colored dog appeared by itself and began barking. Gabriel came out from behind the house, held up his hand to shade his eyes, and then went back out of sight. Tommy imagined it took Gabriel a minute to be sure of each of the two riders who were now in the company of one another.

A brown-and-white goat with low horns and floppy ears stood aside and watched. The goat had yellow, bulging eyes and bony hips, and it seemed unbothered by the passing men and horses.

Raimundo emerged from behind the house, carrying a pitchfork. He held it with the head up as he stopped and said, "*Hola,* Beel."

Lockwood stopped his horse. "*Buenas tardes.* You know this lad here, don't you?"

"Oh, sure. Tomi." Raimundo motioned with his head. "What you got there?"

"I'll let him tell you."

Tommy said, "I killed an antelope, but it's a lot more than I can eat myself. So I thought I'd like to give you a good part of it."

Raimundo's eyes widened. "That's nice you think of us." He gave an uncertain look toward Lockwood and came back to Tommy. "We're sorry to hear about Red. That's a bad thing."

Tommy took a deep breath and tried to keep his voice steady. "Thanks," he said. "It's not an easy thing to deal with. It's hard to . . . understand, I guess."

"I know you were like brothers. I was afraid something happen to you, too."

"No, he was off on his own. I was waitin' for him to come back."

"Well, I'm sorry. My whole family, we're sorry. You got no family, and now even your friend, you lose him."

Tommy's throat was tight. "I just try to get by," he said.

"Sure."

Lockwood spoke in a cheerier tone. "Why don't we get this meat out of the sun?"

"That's a good idea," said Raimundo. "We gonna eat in a little while. We can use some of it right now." He spoke in Spanish to Gabriel, who had come up beside him. Then in English he said, "Here, you let Gabriel take your horses, and we take care of the meat."

"I'll help," said Tommy as he slid down. "We just watered 'em, so I think tyin' 'em up will be good enough."

Lockwood was on the ground, untying the bundle. He spoke with an air of familiarity as he said, "Any more trouble with Cushman?"

"Not yet."

"Well, I don't think he'll do anything while we're here."

"Ha-ha. Maybe you better stay."

Lockwood smiled. "We'll have to see. It wouldn't be the worst idea."

Tommy tied the two horses to the lean-to where he and Red had tied them before. He loosened the cinches and left the horses standing in the shade.

Inside the house, he let his eyes adjust to the dimmer light. The antelope carcass, wrapped in the light canvas sheet, lay on the table. Raimundo sat in his usual place, and Lockwood sat in the place where Red had sat. The two men were smoking cigarettes and had a relaxed air about them. As Tommy approached the table, Lockwood looked around at him.

"I didn't want to take any liberties with your animal," he said, "but I can help you cut some meat if you'd like."

"I can do it myself," said Tommy. He turned to Raimundo. "I'll need a knife and a board."

Raimundo called to the kitchen in Spanish, and a minute later, Milena appeared with a cutting board and a butcher knife. Tommy thanked her, and she went back to the kitchen. Lockwood did not miss a bit of the movement.

Tommy did not want to hold up dinner, so he decided to cut up a hindquarter. Working from memory, he cut around the hip joint and trimmed the leg and thigh free. He set it on the board and went about separating the meat from the bone. After a little more than ten minutes, he had a pile of boned meat. Milena reappeared with a second board and knife, and she joined him in the task of cutting the meat into bite-sized pieces.

Lockwood gave an occasional glance as he continued to chat in a mixture of English and cow-country Spanish. Tommy did not know much Spanish, but he could hear Lockwood's imperfect pronunciation as he knocked the corners off of words and pronounced the *r*'s and *d*'s as he would in English. Thus *carne* came out "carney," *tarde* became "tardy," and *becerro,* the word for calf, was trimmed down to "b'sero." Raimundo took it all in with no reaction, though his clear, crisp intonation made a noticeable contrast.

Milena scraped all of the cut-up meat onto her board and carried it into the kitchen. Tommy figured that dinner was still at least fifteen minutes away, so he went to work on the other hindquarter.

Gabriel came in, and Tommy gave him the first thigh and leg bone to give to the dog. Gabriel returned and watched until the second set of bones was free. After flexing the hinged joint as if the bones were a toy, he took them to the dog as well. By then, the first plate of food arrived, so they set the meat and other items on a wooden armchair in the sitting area.

Milena served all four plates as well as

two stacks of warm corn tortillas. Tommy wished Anita would make an appearance, but by now he was conditioned to take whatever came out of the kitchen. He turned his attention to the antelope meat that was swimming in red chile sauce as the pork had done. The first bite was chewy, but it tasted as if it had been tenderized somewhat by the sauce being cooked into it. He ate one piece after another, chewing and savoring, then began to combine the meat with the beans. He was so hungry and the food was so satisfying that he forgot about the tortillas until he was almost finished with his plate.

Lockwood had made short work of his meal as well.

Milena materialized again from the kitchen and asked the single-word question, *"¿Más?"*

Lockwood flattened out his *r*'s as he said, *"Por favor."*

By the time Milena came back with Lockwood's second serving, Tommy had cleaned his plate. He was ready for her question.

"¿Más?"

He put all he could into his *r*'s as he answered, *"Por favor."*

She brightened and smiled. *"Un momento,"* she said.

Tommy's second plate arrived, and he went at it with a little more leisure. He helped himself to a tortilla. He listened to the conversation between the two men.

He picked up the words for water, dirt, and men. He recognized Cushman's name in its variant pronunciations. Raimundo seemed to be explaining his people's circumstances in a plain way, while Lockwood seemed to be making an effort to make his statements with effect.

Tommy's spirits picked up when he saw both Anita and Milena standing in the kitchen doorway. They were listening to Lockwood. So was Gabriel. Tommy paid attention.

Now with an audience, Lockwood spoke in straight, deliberate English. "It is not right what this man Cushman does. He does not own the water. He may think he does, but it only flows across his property from somewhere else. He may use it, and draw from it, but he does not own it. In higher laws, water belongs to everyone. No one has a right to cut off someone else's water." He pushed his plate away and shrugged, as if to say that it was only his opinion and not well said at that. But the others seemed impressed, as they nodded in agreement. Anita relayed the contents to Milena in Spanish, and Milena nodded as well, saying, *"Pues, sí, es cierto."*

It was a brief moment but a high point as it held the people together. Within a few seconds, they went about their separate activities. Anita and Milena cleared the table and disappeared into the kitchen. Lockwood brought out his cigarette makin's. Tommy and Gabriel put the remainder of the antelope on the table, along with the board and knife.

Tommy severed the two shoulders from the carcass and began to cut out the remaining backstrap. As he did so, Gabriel cut up the hindquarter meat that Tommy had boned before dinner. Tommy took out the backstrap in one long, neat piece and set it aside. It was pleasing to see. He imagined it making about fifteen or twenty nice chops, suitable for pan frying.

He went to work on the shoulder. The meat and tendons were tougher here, and the bones were more difficult. He became absorbed with separating the meat from the shoulder blade and from around the joints. When he looked up, Gabriel had cut up the whole backstrap and put the meat onto the general pile.

Tommy felt an immediate sinking of the spirits, but he figured it was too late to say anything, so he went back to work. The best meat would go into the pot with the toughest, and in the long run it wouldn't make much difference.

Milena came out of the kitchen and traded a clean board for one that was stacked with meat. She said something in Spanish to Gabriel.

Tommy gave him an inquisitive look.

"She says they're going to make *pozole*."

"What's that?"

Gabriel tipped his head as if he was picking the words. "It's like a soup, with meat and onions and corn. Big corn." With his thumb and forefinger he made a circle about the size of a chickpea.

"Are they going to use all the meat?"

"I think so. Cook it all so it doesn't go to waste."

"Just as well, I guess."

Tommy took a seat on the shady side of the house where Raimundo and Lockwood had retired after dinner. The men were smoking cigarettes and drinking liquor out of two small glasses. Across the bare ground, the cauldron was hanging over the fire pit again, and smoke was rising up around the sides. Life had eased into a casual pace, and Tommy let the tension flow away. He closed

130

his eyes and picked up a few stray words from the men's conversation. The aroma of spices and boiling meat drifted on the air. At some time a few hours from now, he would find out what *pozole* was like.

He awoke with a haunting, hollow sense of Red's death. Red had sat in this very place, had smoked cigarettes with Raimundo as Lockwood was doing now. But no more. Never again would Tommy's friend ride a horse, scheme on an unbranded calf, mock the boss, or go after a girl. He was here one moment and gone the next, never to come back. The largeness of it all, the finality, had Tommy in a daze.

Life and its familiar aspects came back to him as he heard the continuous, low-toned conversation between Lockwood and Raimundo. Lockwood commented on how good the tequila was. Raimundo agreed with a casual *"Ah, sí."* Lockwood remarked that the sun was very strong this time of year. Raimundo agreed again. Lockwood said that he thought the *pozole* would be very good. Raimundo said, with more enthusiasm, *"Oh, sí."*

Tommy blinked and opened his eyes wider to look around. Anita and Milena were standing at the large kettle. Milena was stirring the contents with a wooden spoon. Anita gave him a glance and smiled, then took the spoon that Milena handed her. Anita stood up straight and showed nice form as she dipped the spoon into the cauldron, brought it out, and blew the steam off of it. Tommy looked around for Faustino and did not see him. He recalled Gabriel's account of Faustino dropping his interest in Milena as he became fixed on Anita. Tommy smiled at the possible nuances to the situation. Maybe Milena's presence upset the man's composure.

Anita and Milena went inside, and the afternoon emptied again. The shadows began to stretch out. Tommy nodded off and woke up. Raimundo had left, and Lockwood was dozing in his chair. Tommy closed his eyes again.

The evening began to liven up as Gabriel and then Alejo joined the group. Milena set out a wooden box to serve as a table. A minute later she brought a small bowl of dried red chile and a smaller bowl with a dried, crushed herb. Then, with Anita at work with the ladle, she served the bowls of *pozole.* Each man added a spoonful of chile and half a teaspoon of the dried herb. Lockwood seemed at home with the routine and fit right in with the others.

Raimundo pointed with his spoon as he said to Tommy, "Put some *chile*. And *orégano*."

Tommy did as he was told, then sat down and stirred the new ingredients into the soup. The *pozole* consisted of antelope meat, hominy, and cooked onions. The combination was excellent, notwithstanding a slight gamy flavor from the antelope and one mouthful in which he came down on half a clove of garlic.

Everyone ate in silence for a while until Raimundo said, "This is very good."

Lockwood's voice was cheerful. "I can't complain." He smiled as Milena took his bowl for a second serving.

Even Alejo, who had kept an untrusting eye on Tommy most of the time, relented. "Yes, berry good," he said. "You bring good meat."

"He is a good boy," said Raimundo. "He has no family. We are sorry for his friend. May he rest in peace." Turning to Tommy, he said, "This is your house. Like before, you stay with us." Then to Lockwood he said, "You, too."

Lockwood smiled and held up his hand. "I don't want to impose. Besides, I have my own camp." He smiled at Milena as he took the bowl she handed him.

"You go there and get your things."

"We'll see."

Milena served a second bowl to each of the others, and the meal went on in silence.

The fire burned down, and Milena and Anita went inside. The bowls stacked up on the wooden box, and Lockwood brought out his tobacco and papers. Raimundo and Alejo each rolled a cigarette, and as the makin's came back around to Lockwood, everyone looked up to see Faustino, who had appeared in the group like a stranger out of the dusk.

All of the men, including Lockwood, greeted him in Spanish. As if to put himself on a higher plane and to set the mode of the conversation, he answered in English.

"Good evening. Everyone had a good supper?"

"Oh, yes," said Raimundo. "Please have some. *Con confianza.*"

"No, thank you." Faustino was wearing a white shirt and a black vest, with a silver watch chain drooping. He took out the watch, gave it an unhurried glance, and put it away. With a nod each at Tommy and Lockwood, he rested his gaze on Raimundo and said, "I have heard the news of the young American with the red hair."

"It is very sad."

"Yes, and of course, I am sorry for it." Faustino gave another nod to Tommy. "There is nothing good to it. But at least it happened over there."

Tommy stared at the man. Faustino had the face of a man of thirty, with no wrinkles or blemishes but starting to fill out. His skin was smooth, not very dark, and although the flesh on his cheeks and cheekbones looked soft, the set of his mouth and the glint of his eyes expressed a hardness like granite.

Faustino caught Tommy's eyes and moved back to Raimundo. "It is no pleasure to say that I warned of it."

Raimundo took a slow breath and raised his head. "Faustino, if you are trying again to run this boy away, you do not have . . . there is no use. I have told him he can stay with us. He is a guest in my house. And also, he has no family. The boy who was like a brother to him has died. This boy does not cause trouble. He is a worker. Even if he came here with nothing, which he did not, for he brought meat, and he has his own horse, I would not turn him away. To the contrary, I invited him. So he is here to stay with me if he wants to."

Faustino sniffed through his well-trimmed

mustache. "You know as we say in Spanish, that which begins bad ends bad. Trouble follows some people." His gaze took in Lockwood. "And we do not know the motives of some."

Raimundo answered. "And as we also say in Spanish, before you say someone else is a cripple, look at your own feet."

Faustino's face stiffened.

Alejo spoke a full sentence in Spanish. Tommy turned to Gabriel for an explanation.

"He says that my father is older and knows many things, and the younger man should not try to argue with him."

Faustino shifted his feet and continued in English for the benefit of all present. "You are right, uncle. I will not argue with don Raimundo, and I will not fight about a boy." His chest went up and down with a labored breath, and he turned to Lockwood. "I am sure you are just visiting, and I hope you enjoy your stay."

Raimundo said, "Leave him alone."

With full repose as before, Faustino addressed his elder. "Very well. I will say this in general. The American visitor is welcome. Good. He sits around all day talking. Smoking cigarettes and drinking tequila. Good. If this were a village where no trouble happened, he could sit with the other *holga-zanes* and peel peanuts all day long." Faustino's face tightened, and his eyes blazed. "But trouble is going to come, and we need to take care of our people. We don't need a *conchudo* sitting around in the middle of it."

Lockwood stood up. "I know what that word means. If you want to call me a moocher, that's your privilege, here in your own place. But I'll tell you one thing. I pay my own way in life, and I pay for what I break. I thought I might be able to lend a helpin' hand here, but there's nothin' to keep me. I've got my own camp to go back to anyway, so now is just as good a time as any." He gave a tug at his hat brim and turned to Tommy. "You're free to ride along or stay here, either one."

Tommy exchanged a glance with Raimundo and said, "I think I'll stay here with my friends."

"No harm in that." Lockwood turned away and walked to the lean-to with a steady gait.

He came back leading his horse. He stopped a couple of yards away from the gathering and tightened his saddle cinch. Tommy expected someone to say something, if not that he was welcome to stay, at least that he was welcome to come back. No one said anything, though they all stood up, and Lockwood remained nonchalant. He swung into the saddle, touched his six-gun as if by habit to make sure it was settled in place, and reined the grey horse aside. He had put on his buckskin-colored riding gloves, and he cut a good figure as he touched the brim of his dusty black hat.

"So long," he said. He nodded at Tommy and said, "See you later, kid. Take care of yourself."

"Thanks, Bill. Good luck."

As Lockwood rode away in the dusk, Tommy thought Faustino was a fool to run off an ally with a gun.

The sound of voices woke Tommy in his bed in the lean-to. He did not pick out words, but he could recognize the sounds and intonation of Spanish. He rolled out of his bed and sat up.

Across the yard, between the houses and not far from the fire pit, Faustino and his brother formed one side of a conversation with Alejo and Raimundo on the other. The voices went up and down, and Faustino made gestures with his hands. Meanwhile, his brother stood by with his arms folded and his fists pushing out his biceps.

Tommy pulled on his boots and put on his hat. As he was rolling up his bed, Gabriel dropped by in his usual cheerful mood.

"Sounds like they're at it again," said Tommy.

"Faustino says we should all leave. Go away."

Tommy wondered if it was some other strategy to try to get rid of him. "What's his reason?"

"He says Cooshmon has warned us, and now with you here, Cooshmon has even more reason to come and push us."

Tommy let out a breath of exasperation. "He doesn't give up, does he? At least about me. It seems like he's givin' up with Cushman."

"I don't know."

The voices rose, and then the conversation came to an end. The group separated, with Faustino and his brother going in the direction of Faustino's house while Alejo and Raimundo headed toward the Villarreal house. There the two older men stopped and resumed their conversation.

Gabriel left Tommy and stood by his father as the two older men talked. After a couple of minutes, Alejo left for his house, and Raimundo went into his own. Gabriel came back to the lean-to.

"Well, what's going on?" Tommy asked.

"Faustino is going away."

"Really? Is he pulling out?"

"I don't think so. My father says he is going to take care of his own interests, which I think means money. But he wants people to think he is leaving because they will not listen to his good judgment."

"So he's leaving in a sulk. Doesn't he have money that belongs to other people?"

"Some, but he leaves that with Emilio, his brother."

"Does he just want everybody to do things his way?"

"I think so. And he gets jealous when they don't. My father says we see which foot he limps on."

Tommy laughed. "He'll be back, then."

"I think so."

Tommy looked across the empty yard where the men had stood. Maybe he could breathe easy for a while. He would not miss Faustino Romero, and the man's absence might make it easier for him to see more of Anita.

CHAPTER SEVEN

The morning sun glistened on Pete's back as Tommy combed the horse's mane. Chickens clucked as they scratched the earth. The speckled goat and the brown-and-white goat poked around, now and then emitting a low, clear *meh-eh-eh-eh* sound. A sand-colored burro with a dark, striped cross on its neck and shoulder stood at Alejo's back door, as if it was waiting for a crust of bread or a tortilla with a trace of salt. Smoke came from the fire pit, curling up around the sides of the laundry cauldron and drifting on the air. It had a thick, acrid smell that Tommy correlated with the chunks of old posts that Alejo had put on the fire a little earlier.

The back door opened, and Elsa and her mother came out, carrying a basket of laundry between them. The *señora* said, ¡Ay, burro! and pushed the animal on the nose to move it out of the way. Elsa did not look in Tommy's direction. She kept her back to

141

him as she and her mother lifted the garments one by one and dropped them into the pot. After a couple of minutes, they shook out the empty basket and went into the house.

Tommy slipped the small steel comb into his back pocket and took out an oval-shaped brush not much bigger than the palm of his hand. He slipped three fingers through the strap and began brushing Pete's neck.

The back door of the Villarreal house opened, and Tommy felt a wave of pure admiration as Anita stepped into the sunlight. Her long, dark hair was shining and made a pretty contrast with her yellow dress. At her side she carried a tin pail. In a glance Tommy saw onion skin, corn cobs, pieces of corn tortilla, and chile stems. He met Anita's eyes, and she smiled.

"Good morning," she said.

"Good morning." He took off his hat and put it back on, but he thought she missed the gesture as she turned and pitched the scraps out onto the ground.

The chickens came scurrying, and the two goats were not far behind. Then came the sand-colored burro in a lumbering trot. It forged ahead between the two goats, lowering its large head and plowing the two smaller animals aside. The burro curled

142

back its lip, showing big, wide teeth, and settled onto a corn cob. It lifted its head and began chewing the dry cob.

Anita stayed clear of the horse as she took a couple of steps toward Tommy. She raised her hand and brushed her hair in back of her shoulder. In a quiet voice she said, "I'm sorry about your friend. I didn't get a chance to tell you yesterday."

"It's all right. I appreciate you mentioning it. I don't think I've gotten a hold of it yet myself." He ran the brush across Pete's shoulder.

"It's very sad. We knew that he was like a brother to you. And now you are alone."

"I was alone before, but it feels worse now. I didn't have any enemies then, at least that I knew about." He met her eyes. "I appreciate your father inviting me to stay here, but I'm not a helpless kid. All these grown men treat me like one, but I can take care of myself. I can work and pay my own way. I can cook my food. I can wash my own clothes when I need to."

Anita nodded and let him speak on.

"I realize that I am a kid in some ways. I mean, I'm not grown up like your father, or Bill Lockwood, or —" He was about to say "Faustino," but he shifted and said, "or like Vinch Cushman and some of his riders."

143

He brushed along Pete's back, above the ribs. The sorrel coat was shiny. "Not to brag, but I've earned what I've got. I told you that before. To live and work in this country, I need a horse and a rifle and a coat and gloves, plus a bedroll. I have those, and I'm building my way up."

"And you have a pistol."

"Well, yes. I take it out when I need it." He gave Pete a long sweep with the brush. "I saw Elsa a few minutes ago. I didn't see her all day yesterday."

"She stays in the house. She was very sad about Red, also. She was crying. My uncle told her he wasn't worth crying about, because he got himself in trouble. But that just made her cry more."

A feeling of dread diffused through Tommy's upper body. His throat was tight, and he set his teeth as he fought back the tears. "People can say those things," he said.

"My uncle is old-fashioned, very traditional. He doesn't want to be mean, but —"

"I know. Boys are careless, and they get in trouble. I can't deny that Red was that way. It's just too bad that things ended so soon for him."

"Well, we hope he is at peace." Then in a lighter tone she said, "I like your horse. He's pretty, and he seems to fit you well."

"Thanks. I'm kind of proud of him, though he's an older horse." Tommy stood out of the way so that Pete's white blaze and white front socks showed to advantage.

"And he's not a big horse. That's better. I get afraid with the big horses."

"Smaller horses can be trouble, too, of course, but I know what you mean. Seems like sometimes a big horse doesn't see you and wants to back right over you. But it's a matter of the horse. Big ones can be dog-gentle." Tommy smiled. "Just seems like you have to climb a long ways to get on top of 'em."

Anita laughed. "Well, I like this one."

"He's good for me." Tommy patted the horse on the neck. "His name's Pete. I might have told you that before."

"Yes, you did."

"You can pet him if you'd like."

With the pail still in her left hand, she stepped forward and patted the horse on the shoulder. She smiled and stepped back. "I'd better go back in," she said.

Tommy wondered if he should try tipping his hat again, but the scene was interrupted by the sand-colored burro. The animal came up behind Anita and drove his nose down into the pail.

The movement jerked her out of her

graceful posture for a second and turned her until she lowered the pail and swung it away. *"¡Ay, burro!"* she said, in a scolding voice. Then she looked over her shoulder, smiled at Tommy, and resumed her cheerful tone as she said, "Goodbye."

"See you later," he said as he watched her walk away.

He came back to himself and looked around. He expected to see Faustino Romero giving him a disapproving scowl, but no one else was in view. The chickens were pecking away at the scraps, one of the goats was nibbling on an onion skin, the burro with the striped cross was nosing among the chile stems and seeds, and the smoke continued to rise from the fire pit.

Children's laughter carried on the air as Tommy crouched at his job of splitting kindling. The fire beneath the laundry cauldron had burned out. Elsa and her mother had rinsed and hung the clothes, and a woman from a couple of houses over was bathing two of her children in a metal washtub. She dipped water from the cauldron and poured it over the two children, who stood naked in the tub. Tommy took care not to look at the naked children, but the occurrence seemed normal to everyone else, including Gabriel, who was hoeing in the garden patch, and Anita, who crossed the yard and went into the house where Elsa lived. Three other children played nearby, chasing each other and laughing.

Tommy heard a woman's voice and looked up from his work. Milena had come around the front of Alejo's house and was speaking in a commanding tone. Two children, about four and six years old, detached themselves from their game and went to her. She took one by each hand and marched away, looking once in the direction of the creek.

Tommy stood up from his work and walked out to the open area to get a better view. Coming up the slope from the creek was Fred Berwick, once again in the company of Walt McKinney. Tommy's eyes tightened. A second later, two more riders came into view. Tommy did not recognize them. They were heavier built than either Walt or Fred, almost as large as Lew Greer. They could be brothers, Tommy thought. Then he saw that they were riding horses that he and Red used to ride. These would be the two bulldogs Red referred to.

Even at a distance of forty yards, Tommy saw surprise register with Fred Berwick. But the horses did not slack their pace. They came forward at a brisk walk, picking up their feet, until Fred and then Walt came to a stop. The other two riders hung back and stopped as well.

Raimundo and Alejo came out of their respective houses and met where Tommy was standing. Faustino had left earlier on his bay horse, and as far as Tommy knew, the other men of the village were out with the sheep.

Fred did not speak right away. He was clean-shaven and dressed in neat clothes as always, but he had a queasy look about him, as if his mission did not set well with his stomach. Walt had his casual, half-attentive air as he slouched in the saddle and rolled his head from one side to the other. The two bulldogs in back had their brims pulled down against the sun, and so their faces were in shadow.

"Good afternoon," said Fred, looking up as if to be sure of the time of day and then squinting as he refocused.

Raimundo answered. "Good afternoon. In what way can we help you?"

Fred shifted his gaze and put his hands on his saddle horn. His mouth moved one way and then another until he said, "Well, I have another message from Vinch Cushman." He paused, and when no response came, he continued. "He says he thought you should have gotten the idea before, but now he needs to make it clear. The water gets cut off today. You have until the end of the day tomorrow to pack all your things and leave." Fred's voice was quavering, and he pulled in a deep breath. Steadier, he said, "This is Vinch, not me. I'm just delivering the message. But he says that if you people don't leave, something very bad will happen to you, your animals, and your buildings." Fred's eyes swept across the village.

Raimundo made a slow, nodding motion. He lifted his eyebrows and looked square at Fred. "He has to know that whatever he does, sooner or later, he will be in trouble with the law."

Fred shook his head. "I can't tell you what he thinks, because I don't know. Like I say, I'm just the messenger."

"Well, you delivered your message." Raimundo looked at Alejo, gave a small toss of the head, and turned away. Alejo followed.

Fred spoke in a low, matter-of-fact tone. "Tommy. If you've got a minute."

Tommy walked forward a few steps. "I don't know what you —"

"Look, Tommy. This is none of my doing. I'm sorry about what happened to Red. I didn't have anything to do with it. And I don't like being a part of this, either."

"Then why don't you ride away?"

"Why don't you?"

Tommy gave it a second's thought. "I've got different reasons than you do."

"Then let's leave it at that. I didn't come to argue with you, Tommy. I didn't even know you were here. But I'll tell you this. You know how Vinch is. He really has a vendetta against these people. He hates them."

"I know that."

"I mean it. He's serious. I hope they take his warning. For their own good. If they don't want to, I hope you can talk some sense into them."

"No one listens to me, Fred. I'm just a kid."

Fred grimaced as if his stomach was still in turmoil. "Well, just remember. It's nothing personal between you and me."

"I don't know, Fred. As long as you ride for Vinch Cushman and carry his messages, there's got to be something. But I'll try. No hard feelings."

"Thanks, Tommy. And good luck." Fred reined his horse around and made a clucking sound.

Walt McKinney sat up straight, bringing his yellow-handled cross-draw pistol into view where it rode in its holster. He gave Tommy a slight glance as he turned his horse and fell in with Fred. The two of them rode down the slope past the other two riders, who waited and then walked their horses around to form the rear guard. None of the four men looked back.

Tommy stood alone on the bare ground, letting the importance of the moment sink in. Vinch Cushman had drawn a line in the sand, as the saying went. As Tommy reviewed Fred's words about how much Vinch hated these people, he wondered whether Vinch would be satisfied with running them off.

Faustino Romero returned to the village in the evening while the people were in a bustle packing up their possessions. Tommy noted an expression of great displeasure as the man stopped his horse and looked down at those around him. He had crossed the creek and had no doubt seen that the water had quit flowing. Now he sat with his gloved hands on his wide, wooden pommel as Alejo spoke to him in Spanish in a curt tone. Tommy had the impression that among the circumstances that displeased Faustino, one was that he had not been present when the people had agreed among themselves to leave. But he himself had spoken in favor of leaving, and any moment for debate had long passed. Now was the time to decide what the people could take with them and what they would have to leave behind.

Raimundo's family was as busy as all the others. Tommy had offered the services of his horse, and Raimundo said Milena needed help the most. She had no horse or wagon, and her old burro had been killed. The other families were sharing their carts and wagons and burros and horses, so anything Tommy could carry for Milena would mean less of a burden for the others. Raimundo also mentioned, in an incidental way, that two of the wagons and three of the horses belonged to the Romero brothers, which left Tommy to interpret that Milena was pushed that much more to the side.

For the time being, then, Tommy did not have much to do. He was sure, however, that Faustino regarded him as a loafer.

The first herd of sheep arrived at the village in the middle of the morning. Two men whom Tommy had seen only in passing left the sheep on the eastern edge of the village with Gabriel and another boy his age to watch them. As they stopped on their way back for the second bunch of sheep, Tommy noted their bony horses and worn saddles. He offered to go with the men, but they said they did not need any help. They ate a quick meal standing by their horses, then left the village on a jolting trot.

To make himself useful, Tommy saddled Pete and rode out to the ground where the sheep were grazing. The first thing that struck him was that the sheep were all faced the same way, and the second was that they were dirtier and greyer than he expected them to be when he got up close. He rode around the herd, but with fewer than a hundred head and all of them grazing to the northeast, he did not have much to do. When he rode around to Gabriel's side, he dismounted and chatted.

Gabriel explained the plan. The people would drive their animals and haul their possessions a few miles east to get out of Cushman's reach and to wait until someone came to restore law and order. Faustino would go for help as soon as the people got settled in a new camp.

Tommy went back to the village, and the place was buzzing. Hammers banged as people nailed together crates, boxes, and pens. Voices traveled back and forth. Chickens squawked as people caught them and caged them. A hog was squealing and grunting as one man held it by the hind legs and another man was taking aim with an ax.

Tommy reported to Raimundo, who told him he could help with the hog butchering. Alejo and another man were killing two half-grown pigs rather than try to drive them. They didn't have enough water to scald two pigs, so they were skinning them. Tommy tied up his horse and walked back to the scene of the slaughter. He told the men that Raimundo had sent him to help, so they put him to work skinning one of the pigs.

Noise came from all around. Hammers continued to bang. Women hollered at children. Men called out questions and answers. A child cried. Chickens cackled in their cages, and one of the goats began to bleat. Hurry was on the air, while a sense of urgency and worry spread at a lower level.

The pigskin was tight, and every quarter-inch of it had to be trimmed away with a knife. Tommy learned to lay his knife blade flat against the carcass and cut through the layer of fat with steady strokes. There would be no saving of this skin for *chicharrones,* nor would there be time to render the lard.

A donkey began to bray. A dog yelped as the man skinning the other pig kicked at the dog and shouted. A woman's high-strung voice cried, *"¡Ay, Fidel!"* in the tone of a mother complaining to a child. In the short time that Tommy had lived among the people, he had become used to hearing someone, somewhere in the village, singing. But no one was singing today. No one was happy.

People were loading their possessions into carts and wagons when the second herd of sheep passed by the edge of the village. Tommy caught a whiff of the pungent, greasy odor. The two men on horses drove the sheep, with the help of two dogs. Farther back, a man with a burro and a pack came hoofing along with the lead rope in one hand and a herding stick in the other.

Milena brought out two large canvas bags with loop handles of cotton rope. As Tommy hoisted the first one to tie it onto his saddle, he realized it was a small pannier, about the size someone would use on a packsaddle for a donkey. He recalled the grey burro that he and Gabriel had found at sundown a few days earlier, and he thought, this was the way things went with a woman who had lost her man — one step at a time, downhill. He thought she handled it rather well, as if she was going on a trip and was getting her things into the baggage car. He couldn't help feeling a tinge of contempt for Faustino Romero, but when it came right down to it, Faustino had no obligation to take care of her just because she was a widow and he was the one single man in the village.

Tommy tied the two panniers across, then snugged his own gear on top. He had not done much with pack animals, and his knots were not those of a packer, but he knew the general rule of keeping the weight balanced and loading it high on the animal.

People were piling their belongings high on the wagons and carts and roping down the loads. Everything went into the vehicles, from clothes and bedding to kitchen utensils to burlap bags of dried red chiles to mops and brooms. Axes and shovels and crowbars went in as well, but brooms seemed the most numerous. Tommy wondered if the people thought they were going to a place where they would have floors to sweep or if they had faith that they would come back to this village and sweep again.

The sun was slipping in the west when the noise began to lessen and the tone of some voices changed. A couple of wagons were ready to go. Tommy could not see where anything was organized or anyone was in charge. But things began to move. A

wagon pulled by one of the bony sheepherder horses rolled first, followed by a dark
burro pulling a cart. A chicken coop was
tied to the back of the cart, and a black-
and-brown goat followed on a tether.

Tommy waited as Raimundo and his wife
stuffed a few more kitchen items among the
blankets and clothes. A child standing by a
nearby wagon would not stop crying. When
Anita came around the side of the wagon
near him, he asked why the child was crying.

"The cat," said Anita. "The cat went to
hide. They have to leave without it."

Tommy still did not feel any sense of order
in terms of people coordinating their efforts
or agreeing who left when. When the Villarreal wagon was ready to go, it moved out,
drawn by the dull-brown horse. The speckled goat and the brown-and-white goat
pranced along behind, each tied by a rope,
and the light-colored dog trotted by the
front wheel. Tommy walked with Pete right
behind his shoulder. Milena walked on the
other side of the wagon, carrying a pack on
her back and holding a child with each
hand. Anita walked with her, also carrying a
pack. Raimundo and Eusebia sat on the
wagon seat. Eusebia looked back at the village and crossed herself.

Gabriel had set out earlier, with the other boy and two men, to move the sheep. The herd was a mile ahead, a slow-moving, greyish-white mass in the afternoon sunlight.

People were still hollering at one another in the village as they finished tying down their loads. Tommy heard their voices, but he did not look back. He did not want to feel guilty for leaving before they did, even though they would not have accepted his help if he had offered. He also did not look back because he thought it would be bad luck.

The last wagon came dragging into camp as the night grew dark. It took its place near the others, but as the camp did not have any definite formation, the layout was a matter of where the people unhitched the animals and dropped the tongue. The camp area was strewn with bundles and bags that people had carried, items they had taken out of the wagons for the night, and a few packs that had been carried on the backs of burros. Each family had its own little space, and the group had a larger common area where most of them gathered around a fire. Raimundo and Alejo, who had seemed to be the keepers of the wood in the village, had brought along a supply of firewood.

Tommy could feel the anxiety and the fatigue that ran through the people, yet he was impressed by their cheerfulness as they sat around the fire. Faustino and his brother had set up two large cast-iron skillets and were frying quantities of cut-up pork. The tantalizing aroma drifted on the air along with smoke from the fire. As people passed around plates of fried meat and stacks of heated tortillas, they exchanged comments in a friendly tone.

Not everyone sat around the fire. Some stayed in their little campsites and ate from their own store of food, and others took hot food from the fire back to their families. No one seemed concerned about where the food came from or where it went. Tommy assumed the meat came off of one of the two pigs he had helped butcher, and he could see that it was being served in liberal portions. Twice he had taken a count of the people, and each time he had come up with twenty-seven in addition to himself. Judging from the rate at which the *pozole* had disappeared, he thought they would be down to the ribs of the first pig by this time tomorrow.

The fire burned down as people had their fill and the skillets were set aside. The embers were beginning to fade and ash over. Eusebia and her sister, Alejo's wife, held hands and began to sing a song. It had a slow melody and a mournful tone, and some of the others joined in. The only words Tommy understood were *Santa Maria,* but he felt the spirit, if not the message, of the song. He felt as if he joined the people in an appeal for consolation and comfort in a time of sadness.

When the song was ended, a muttering began to spread from the smaller groups by the wagons to the larger group around the dying campfire. Everyone had turned to the west, where a glow along the rim of the prairie was visible from a long ways off. It was the glow of a large fire, and it held the people's attention. Tommy picked out the words *pueblo, casa,* and *Cooshmon.* The faces that had been almost happy for a little while looked stricken now, and tears appeared in the eyes of the two sisters who had sung the beautiful song.

Tommy estimated that the group had traveled between eight and ten miles that afternoon. People would be able to see a fire at that distance, especially a good-sized conflagration with plenty of fuel. Tommy formed a picture of the weathered salvage lumber, yellow inside, crackling as the flames leaped. He imagined a large black bird in the background, flapping its wings. Cooshmon. The *zopilote.* The man full of hatred.

By the time Tommy settled into his bed-roll, a light breeze had come in from the west. It carried the smell of smoke. Cushman, or probably his men, had not wasted any time. Tommy tensed as he pulled himself together under his blankets, chilled on a warm summer night.

Chapter Eight

Tommy sat in the shade of his horse and leaned on the two stuffed panniers. He had taken off the packs to give his horse a rest at midday, but with no water to spare and no appreciable grass in the place where they stopped, Pete would have a rest and not much more. So it went with the dull-brown horse of the Villarreals. He stood tied to a wagon wheel with his head hanging low. Raimundo, Eusebia, and Anita sat in the shade of their wagon, as did Milena and her two children. The family seemed incomplete, with Gabriel off tending the sheep. The scene was quiet and morose, as no one spoke, and no other wagons had stopped nearby.

Energy seemed at a low ebb for the group as a whole. After the flurry and nervousness of packing things up and then the push to travel as far as possible the first day, the burning of the village had knocked the wind out of the people. Tired and demoralized, they straggled from camp that morning and strung out their caravan across the rangeland. The grass was poor, losing a slow battle with sagebrush, soapweed, prickly pear, and rabbit brush. Now at midday, paused in the middle of a vast expanse, Tommy could not see a tree in any direction.

He understood that about ten miles east of their first camp, they expected to find a creek that flowed from the north. All of the horses and burros had been pressed into service as draft animals, so no one was at liberty to ride ahead and verify.

The people moved on in their desultory way, each group at its own speed. They did not stop together for a rest. Instead, one wagon passed another and then was passed in turn.

In the later afternoon, dark clouds gathered in the west. Tommy wondered how much a good downpour would do, as they did not have roofs or rain barrels, but even a freshness in the air and a settling of the dust would be welcome. He looked over his shoulder every few steps for more than an hour, but the clouds did not hold together and travel east. Rather, the bank of clouds separated, with one formation moving northeast and the other mass veering to the southeast. An hour after the clouds diverged, the sky cleared up, and dry sunlight poured on the travelers again.

The sun was slipping in the west when Tommy and the rest of the Villarreal group crawled over a low rise and headed down the slope toward water. The two wagons belonging to the Romero brothers had already reached the creek, and Faustino was holding the three horses at the water while they drank.

Raimundo eased his wagon down the hill and positioned it about a hundred yards to the left of, or upstream from, the Romero camp. By the time Tommy had Pete unpacked and unsaddled, Alejo's wagon had pulled in and dropped anchor some ten yards to the left. Household items spilled out of both wagons onto the area in between. Eusebia and her sister sat next to each other on two rolls of bedding and began cleaning dried red chiles that they took out of a burlap sack. They tore off the stems and the shriveled, discolored tips. The women spoke in a normal tone, not agitated and not depressed. Tommy waited until Raimundo had the brown horse unharnessed, and then he led the two horses to water.

As he stood waiting for the horses to drink, he turned and saw that Anita had followed him with the two goats. Faustino had finished with his horses and was tying them up. Meanwhile, his brother Emilio was scraping out a fire pit with a heavy field hoe. Anita ignored them as she walked past their camp, and she smiled at Tommy as she came to a stop at the edge of the stream.

"There's not much water," she said.

"We did well by getting here when we did."

"You've been a good help to Milena."

"It's not much. I'd feel sorry for her, but she doesn't seem to want anyone to feel that way."

"Her husband, José, was very competent. So she is not used to having to depend on others."

"She has pride, all right. In a good way." After a few seconds he said, "I guess everyone here does. This is no place for people who don't."

Anita made a mild frown. "Who would they be, the ones with no pride?"

Tommy shrugged. "Oh, I don't know all of 'em. But people like drunks and deadbeats, or people who have sunk so low that they've given up. I've seen a few. And then there's those who'll do anything just to get on the good side of someone else. I've seen a few of them, too."

"You have seen quite a bit, then?"

"I wouldn't say that. I haven't been to a big city. But I've worked for other people, and I've been to a few towns, so I've met people like the ones I mentioned. A fella who works for low wages and does low work is going to meet low people."

Her eyes had a thoughtful expression as she tipped her head and said, "Do you think people have it in their destiny to be that way?"

He wondered if she was translating her idea from a Spanish version. "Do you mean that they're fated to become that way, or that they've got no choice but to stay that way?"

"Maybe both."

"I don't know. Like I said before about my uncle, he believed that he was stuck, that he was born that way and wouldn't ever get out. So maybe some people are like that — you know, destined. But if there's one thing we're supposed to be able to believe in in this country, it's that we have a chance to do better. Maybe some people have it in their blood to be low. Some of them sure seem that way. But I think, and I sure hope, that if a person has the desire, he can raise himself up at least a little way. The cook at the Muleshoe said you can't make a silk purse out of a sow's ear, which I guess means that if someone's born a certain way, you can't change his nature. The cook had other sayings, too, like 'As is bent the twig, so grows the tree,' but then he would turn around and talk about a diamond in the rough." At her uncertain expression, he said, "You know, like a diamond that has good natural quality but needs to be polished and refined."

"I see."

He went on. "I think there's too much to know about for someone like me. Being young, I mean. Like what is destiny and what things we can choose or change. But I hope I'm not wrong when I say what I did, that I believe that a person who starts out at the bottom can do better for himself. If I couldn't believe that, then I would be low." He laughed. "I feel like I'm going in a circle. I'd better quit." As he looked at her, so pretty, it occurred to him that she might have ideas, too. He said, "What about you? What do you think?"

Her voice was calm as she said, "We believe that everything happens because of God's will. That means good things and bad. Like the burning of our houses, or what happened to Red. But we also believe that everyone has to try to do the right thing, even though we are all sinners."

"How about people who are just low, like the ones I mentioned?"

"Some of that comes from what people want to do. My father says it is the nature of people to want to be like brutes. And they invent things to help them be that way, like whiskey and guns."

Tommy recalled a pleasant image of Raimundo sitting in the shade with Bill Lockwood. "What about tequila?" he asked.

Anita smiled. "I know what you mean. A little bit doesn't make men into brutes. But it is true. Where we come from, there are many strong drinkers among the Mexican people. When we came here, my father and my uncle tried to make sure we didn't bring any of them with us."

"It's something to look out for, all right. From what I've seen, whiskey can bring out the worst in a man." He thought for a second. "But I guess he has to have it in him to begin with. And even at that, if he's got it in him, he might not need whiskey to bring it out." He pictured again the scene at the railroad camp, with coarse men looking on as Red took the money and threw back his head and laughed.

"You have a look of pain on your face," she said.

"Oh. I'm sorry. I was thinking of something that happened one time." In her presence, he felt the urge to confess. He said, "Actually, something I did."

Her eyes widened. "Something bad?"

"Not terrible. But not good. It was something I went along with, and it was against the law." Now he was afraid of what she would think. He said, "That's probably as much as I need to say. But it's something I don't want to do again — that, or anything like it. I guess that's why I was saying earlier that I hoped a person could change for the better."

"Oh, yes," she said, with the sunlight shining on her dark hair as she nodded. "You can't change the way God made you, but you can change the things you do. The thing you talk about, it's in the past." The two goats had finished drinking and were tugging on the ropes. "I need to take these back," she said. "They want to find some grass."

"I need to do the same," he said, glancing at the horses. They were still drawing in from the thin flow of water. "I'll see you later. They're not quite done."

"All right."

169

Tommy watched her walk away with the two goats in the lead, straining. He turned to take in more of the camp, and he saw Faustino pause in his work of setting rocks in the fire pit. Tommy looked away. He did not like Faustino ogling, and he did not like himself seeing it.

The camp held together in its loosely structured way as it had done the evening before. Dogs, goats, children, and an occasional burro wandered among the wagons as the adults sat in small groups and chatted. The sheep were strung along the creek, crowding in bunches. Smoke drifted on the air, and as night fell, the two large skillets became hot enough that the aroma of fried pork began to drift out. People congregated at the fire as meat came out of the skillets and was portioned out.

Tommy ate his fill, noting again that the Mexicans never begrudged a person a plate of food. Individual families were cleaning up the last of leftover rice, beans, corn tortillas, and garden vegetables. For his own part, in addition to the cooked pork, Tommy had a shriveled green pepper and a couple of half-grown onions.

When the skillets came off the fire, Emilio covered the grate with a layer of pork ribs.

With his thumb and fingers he spread on salt, pepper, and a third spice that wafted on the warm air and smelled like an herb. Tommy guessed it was the oregano he had heard of earlier, with the *pozole.* Before long, the pleasing smell of roasting fat, combined with the seasonings, gave a sense of being in a big dining hall or at an outdoor occasion like a wedding. With a long knife and a longer roasting fork, Faustino lifted the cooked pieces and set them on plates that people held forward. No one crowded, and no one complained. In the end, the grate was left empty with thin smoke rising as the last of the embers cooked off the grease. Faustino and Emilio stood side by side, each picking a rib bone.

Gabriel had come in from tending the sheep. He was sitting cross-legged next to Tommy and eating from a plate his mother had saved for him.

Tommy said, "What's the plan for tomorrow?"

"I think we stay here one day, to rest and to let all the animals eat grass. It takes a day to cook beans and make tortillas."

"And after that?"

"Oh, I don't know. That's in the future. But we need to find more water than we have here."

The people had drifted back to their smaller groups, and all of the dogs had disappeared with their bones. Faustino lifted the grate from the fire pit, leaned it on a low, smooth stone, and walked away with his brother. An orange glow showed through the embers as a layer of ash formed on the surface. A low, even tone of people talking in Spanish came from different directions.

Tommy stared up at the sky and saw the same stars as always. They looked down on every place he had been — Nebraska, the Muleshoe, the White Wings Ranch, the Mexican village, and now this spot out in the middle of a vast rangeland, camped with twenty-seven other people and a hundred sheep, on the edge of a thin little stream with poor grass all around. It seemed to him that he worried more about the past and about the future than these other people did. He would like to know what to expect for the day after tomorrow, on the other side of the creek, just as he would like to know how much of his past was going to determine his future. He hoped he wasn't fated to be a poor man with a poor way of doing things. At least he wasn't running from his past, as he had known of others. If he was, this would be a slow way of doing it.

■ ■ ■ ■

The fried pork for breakfast weighed heavy in Tommy's stomach, and the smell of grease struck him as being stronger than the night before. He was used to side pork or bacon in the morning, but the cow outfits usually had spuds or biscuits to go along, to soften or absorb the grease. He reminded himself that this was food, and he was glad to have it.

After Tommy handed his plate to Gabriel to be set in the dishpan, Raimundo spoke from where he sat on the ground nearby.

"Today, the women cook beans, and they boil corn for tortillas. We're gonna use all the wood this morning, so you boys have to go look for some."

Tommy said, "I haven't seen any trees at all. How about if we gather sagebrush? It doesn't make a big fire, but it burns all right."

Raimundo smiled. "You need a lot, and you don't carry it very well on a horse. I think you need a canvas, and bring it back in a ball."

"In a bundle. We can do that. Tie the corners together."

"Yeah, try that. They wanna start early

with the cookin'. You get some sagebrush, then maybe you go look for wood."

Finding sagebrush was not hard, but finding enough dead stuff for a day's worth of cookfires was going to be slow work. With one corner of the canvas tied by a length of rope to each saddle horn, the horses dragged the tarpaulin between them. The boys gathered faggots and tossed them on, one by one. The dead branches were an inch thick at the best and dwindled into twigs after a foot or less. The pile grew, and the boys tromped it down. It grew more, and pieces began to roll off the back end. Now the boys had to squash down the load more often. After a couple of hours, they had enough for a full bundle. They tied the four corners together, boosted the unwieldy load onto Pete's saddle, and tied it down.

Back in camp, half the load disappeared in the time that Tommy and Gabriel ate a bowl of oatmeal mush. The sun had climbed well past midmorning when they set out for the next load.

On the first excursion they went north. The second time, they traveled northwest, where it looked as if the sagebrush grew thicker. Up close, however, the pickings were sparse as ever, with a dead branch here and another one there. The pile grew at a petty pace like before, and by the time they had a full load, they had a two-mile walk back to camp.

Anita, Elsa, and Milena were in charge of boiling the corn. They were glad to see more fuel. So were the women cooking the big pot of beans. Faustino and Emilio, who were apparently saving themselves for the more prestigious job of cooking the meat, were snoozing under their two wagons. A cheerful mood drifted around the camp, with children laughing and the women at the cook pots talking in their singsong cadence. The aromatic scent of burning sagebrush mingled with the steam that floated off the boiling pots.

Tommy stood next to Anita and said, "What do you call this corn in Spanish?"

"*Maíz,*" she said.

"My-eece."

"Pretty close."

He nodded in the direction of the pot of beans. "And those are *frijoles*?"

"That's right."

"And the firewood?"

"*Leña.*"

"That's a nice word. It sounds like it should be somebody's name." He felt the sound as he repeated the word. "*Leña.* And how do you say 'moon'?"

"Luna."

"That's right. I'd heard it before, but couldn't quite remember. *Luna, leña.*"

"That's good. You're learning it."

"One word at a time. Before long, I'll be talkin' as good as Bill Lockwood."

She laughed. "Oh, yes. You can tell he enjoys it. Very . . . um, not funny, but very . . . nice." Again she seemed to be searching for a word in English to express a thought she had in Spanish.

Milena had turned at the mention of Lockwood's name.

Tommy said, "I hope I didn't say anything wrong."

"Oh, no," said Anita. "We like him. He is very likeable."

"Well, who knows if we'll see him again. I wouldn't be surprised."

After they had rolled up the canvas and watered the horses, Tommy and Gabriel sat in the shade of the Villarreal wagon. The sun had passed over the high point, and the shadows were beginning to grow. Tommy took off his hat and fanned himself.

"I think we should try going south for firewood," he said. "I didn't see anything like a tree all the time we were out north of here."

Gabriel said, "Where there's water, you

176

find trees."

"That's true, but this little creek flows down from there, and I didn't see even a tall bush sticking up."

Raimundo appeared from around the corner of the wagon. "Yeah. You go south. Maybe you'll find something."

Eusebia showed up a couple of minutes later with two bowls of beans. As she handed one to Gabriel, she said something in Spanish. She gave the second bowl to Tommy, accepted his thanks, and walked away.

Gabriel said, "They don't have any tortillas. They need to finish boiling the corn, then grind it, then press the tortillas. Maybe for supper."

"Fine with me." Tommy tried a spoonful from his bowl. All it consisted of was boiled beans and a pinch of salt. But it, too, was food.

South of camp, the stream flowed at a bare trickle, which did not surprise Tommy when he thought of the number of humans and animals taking water from it. He did not think it ran much water even in good times. The course did not cut one way or the other, or leave sandbars, or give rise to anything bigger than bullberry bushes. After a couple of miles of not finding firewood, and seeing no trees anywhere ahead, Tommy suggested that they double back.

Something inside him had told him, all day long, that it wasn't time to cross the creek or do anything to the west. So he circled around to the east as he led the way back toward camp.

Out of habit he scanned the ground ahead, always on the lookout for snakes and for gopher or badger holes. Also, as a matter of course, he kept an eye out for cattle or any sign of them. Wherever cattle grazed, they left hoofprints, cow pies, and broken twigs on the brush. Today he had not seen any recent signs of that nature. The part of the country where they were tarrying seemed empty. Now that he thought of it, he had not seen an antelope or a jackrabbit all day, either. As for the lack of cattle, that was not so bad, he figured. Where there were cattle, there were men checking on them. Maybe the Mexican people would be able to hole up in a place where they wouldn't be bothered until they could find some authority to help them reclaim their land.

The air was growing heavy in the warmest part of the day, and a drowsiness began to settle on Tommy. From time to time a grasshopper clicked and whirred away, causing Pete to break stride and lift his head, but for the rest of the time, Pete seemed to be drowsing along as well. As the ground flowed along beneath the horse's feet, Tommy saw things and then registered them in a delayed reaction.

He stopped the horse. He had seen something. Blinking his eyes and opening them wide, he reined the horse around. He backtracked thirty yards and button-hooked again. He picked up his own trail and followed it, studying the ground as it passed beneath him. There it was. In a patch of rabbit brush, three balls of horse manure had begun to dry and crust over. A horse on the move, but not very fast, had dropped some road apples where there was no road.

Tommy swung down from the saddle and bent over to study the scene all around him. Some of the twigs of rabbit brush had been crushed by horse hooves, and palm-sized patches of bare ground showed nicks. Someone on a horse had been riding from west to east.

Gabriel came plodding back on the brown horse. "What is it?" he asked.

"Nothing much. Just that someone came by here on a horse. Sometime earlier today."

Gabriel wrinkled his nose. "Out here?"

"Sure did. But we're out here, too, so

whoever it is, I guess he's got a reason."

"Hah. Who do you think it is?"

Tommy looked around at the empty land. "I'd like to think it was Bill Lockwood, but it could be anybody. Well, not anybody. Not the queen of England, and probably not cannibals."

"Cannibals? People who eat other people?"

Tommy laughed. "It's from a story I read when I was in school. It's called *Robinson Crusoe*. He gets shipwrecked on an island. After he's there by himself for twenty years, one day he's walking along the beach, and he sees a footprint in the sand. It's a big moment for him. All of a sudden he realizes he's not alone on the island, that he's not safe anymore. So he keeps watch, and sure enough, the cannibals come."

"*¡Válgame!* And they have a fight?"

"They sure do. He has a gun, so he kills a couple of them and rescues another one that they were going to kill and eat. It happens on a Friday, so he calls this man Friday. After that, Friday becomes his loyal servant."

Gabriel laughed. "That's a good story, but I don't think it happens around here."

"Oh, no. It was a long time ago, and it happened on an island down by South

America. It was fiction, of course. It didn't really happen."

Tommy was watering the horses just before sunset when Anita showed up with the two goats. His heartbeat picked up, and he felt a glow, even though it was subdued by the presence of the Romero brothers not far away. As he noted their presence, he thought Anita might have chosen to water the goats when Tommy was there, just to put a damper on Faustino's interest. The thought made him feel better.

"Good afternoon," she said.

"Good afternoon. It's good to see you."

She smiled. "My brother said you read a story about cannibals."

Tommy laughed. "It was about a man who lived all by himself on an island. Just a little of the story was about cannibals. He talks about his goats as much as he does about the savages."

"He has goats?"

"In the story. They live on the island, too. He captures some of them, and he makes them his."

"Did you like the story?"

"Oh, yes. It's a good story for boys, all about this man who lives alone and has to do things for himself."

"Until he has a cannibal for a slave?"

Tommy laughed. "Oh, no. He's an Englishman. His man Friday is more like a servant. He learns to speak proper English, and he goes back to England with his master. But the best part is when Robinson Crusoe lives alone, like a king on his own little island, and does everything for himself."

"Is that what you want, to be alone?"

He laughed again. "Not at all. But the part about being independent — that's good to read. He has his own world, his own system to run. He raises wheat and grapes, and he builds fences for protection. Like I said, it's a good story for boys."

"Did this man write any stories for girls?"

"I think he wrote one about a woman, but the teacher said that was not a good one for us to read."

Supper came together in an agreeable way. Two of the men from the group had gone upstream and had dragged back a dead tree about twelve feet long and almost a foot wide at the base. They chopped it into firewood and split the thickest pieces. Faustino and Emilio cooked up the last of the pork, including the ribs. Everyone had at least one serving of beans along with three or four fresh corn tortillas. After the meal, as the coals still glowed, the people around the fire began to sing songs. Some were lively, and some were slow and mournful. Tommy could pick out only a word here and there, but he gathered that the songs were about pretty girls, beloved horses, and lost love.

Raimundo kneeled by Tommy's side and put his hand on his shoulder. "You can see we are a happy people," he said. "Just a little while, and things will be right again. Don't be sad."

Tommy glanced at the glow of the firelight on Anita's face as she sat between her mother and Elsa and joined in the singing. He said, "I'm not sad, and I'm glad the people are singing." He did not say he was happy, though, because he wasn't. His thoughts were off to the south in the sunny afternoon, when he had seen the footprint in the sand.

Chapter Nine

Camp was slow in stirring the next morning. Tommy expected the people to be gathering up their things and making ready for the next move. As he ate a cold tortilla smeared with a pasty jam he did not recognize, Raimundo told him that two burros had gone missing. No one had seen either of them since the evening before.

"What color are they?" Tommy asked.

"One is the tan one with the cross, and the other is dark, like black, with a white nose and belly. You've seen them both."

"Oh, yeah. I remember them. Do you want me to go out and look for them?"

"You and Gabriel can go south. Another two men can go north. The burros, they probably just go to look for something to eat."

"The grass isn't very good here, so they might have wandered quite a ways."

"I know. Maybe they're together, and

maybe they go different ways."

"Well, we can sure try to find 'em."

"Oh, and one other thing. We use up all the firewood, and a lotta beans and corn, so Milena's big bags can go in the wagon."

Tommy wondered what that meant for him, but not finding a hint, he said, "That's good." He stood up and brushed off the seat of his pants. "I'll get my horse ready, and we'll go look for the donkeys."

By the time he had Pete saddled and watered, Gabriel had the tired-looking brown horse ready to go. Tommy said, "I hope we find better grass in the next place. These fellas didn't get all that much to eat yesterday. I'm not surprised that those two donkeys wandered off." He did wonder why no one had tied up the two animals when the group was on the move like this, but he had become used to the way the people did things, and he knew he would do no good by complaining now.

The two boys headed out of camp as the sun was beginning to warm the morning. Pete snorted and stepped along like a good cow pony, but the brown horse tended to lag, and Gabriel had to kick him every so often so that he would trot and catch up. A mile from camp, Tommy suggested that they split up. Gabriel drifted to the left, and

Tommy struck out to the right, headed southwest. The country was flat, with low-lying brush as he had noticed the day before. The terrain sloped downward for about a mile ahead of him, and then it rose again into rolling country. By himself, and more alert in the morning than he had been the day before in the drowsy heat of the afternoon, he realized that the low area must be where the creek flowed from the Mexican settlement and the White Wings Ranch. He thought he might have ridden across the dry streambed in the afternoon without noticing. It also occurred to him that an animal might find better grass there, as he had discovered with the antelope. The green grass and flowing water of that day now seemed a long time ago, but there might be dry grass somewhere along here.

He found the streambed, and he could not remember crossing it or anything that looked like it the day before. The grass was nothing remarkable, being sparse and dry and cropped close to the ground. Tommy dismounted to look closer, to see if he could find the tracks of a horse, or cattle, or a lost donkey, or even an antelope. Any sign was interesting, and he needed to practice reading that sort of thing.

He walked along bent over, with his reins

186

in his hands. He wondered if a better tracker would see things that he didn't. He tipped his head so that his hat brim cut out the glare of the sun. Both red and black ants were going about their day's work, as were the dry-backed, charcoal-grey beetles. A yellow-orange velvet ant disappeared under a tuft of grass, and a tiny white bone lay by itself in the bare soil.

The ground felt dry and hard beneath his feet, and yet, by his figuring, water had run through here some four days ago. Maybe this was another stream that dried up earlier and not the one he thought it was. He knelt and scratched at the dirt. The dry, caked earth did not give but rather crammed under his fingernail. He pushed with his thumb. Still hard. He decided to stand up and dig with the heel of his boot, but as he did, he felt a terrible hand clamp down on the back of his neck.

His blood went cold. A chill ran through his neck and shoulders. He heard the rustle of clothing, like canvas or denim, and he felt a fleck of saliva on his face as the hand pulled him upward and he heard a deep voice he knew well.

"And what are you doing here, you little son of a bitch?"

He turned to see the shadowed face of

Vinch Cushman — the blotchy, flushed complexion and the stubbled jaw, the beak nose, one eye larger than the other, both of them bleary with the whites yellowed. His head hung forward, and the shadow on his face came from his large, floppy-brimmed hat. He looked bigger than ever against the pale blue sky, his hunched form shrouded with a dark cape of a dustcoat.

The claw-like hand bit into the back of Tommy's neck, then released, and, in less than the blink of an eye, Cushman had him by the front of his shirt and pulled him closer. Spit flew again, and yellow teeth showed. "I said, what are you doing here?"

Tommy's mouth was dry, and he had a hard time swallowing. His heart was pounding. "Out looking . . ." He was thinking *burro* and trying to say *donkey.*

"Out looking for what?"

"A donkey. Two donkeys."

"Puh!" A small spray flew out. "You just as well be lookin' for a titty." Cushman switched hands on Tommy's shirt and pushed back his dustcoat, revealing a dark-handled six-gun. Tommy thought he was going to draw the gun, but instead he lifted a quirt that hung on the handle. He let the coat fall back into place, then slapped the quirt against his coat where it lay along his leg. "Now, tell me, what in the hell are you doin'?"

Tommy felt like a little boy with a whimper in his voice. "I'm helping the Mexicans look for a couple of donkeys."

"I bet you are." Cushman slapped the quirt again. "Now you listen to me. I could leave you here, dead as a jackrabbit, and no one would know the difference. The only reason I don't is to put the fear of God into you." The fist tightened as it twisted Tommy's shirt. "You're a mewling, puking little bastard, is what you are. Probably a runaway, but that doesn't matter to me." The larger eye glared. "All the time you were workin' for me, I thought you and your crooked little friend pulled something, and I would like to have hung you for it. But I didn't catch you at it." Cushman took a deep, wheezing breath. "That was my only regret in firin' the two of you. If you'd stayed on, I might have caught you at something. But your pal got what was comin' to him after all."

Tommy tried not to look at Cushman's face, but he couldn't stand to look at any other part of him. He loathed the man's presence.

"So it wouldn't surprise me if you were out lookin' for somethin' to steal now,

189

'specially since you're out of a job."

"I told you, I'm staying with the Mexicans."

"And I don't doubt it. But that doesn't mean you aren't lookin' for somethin' to make off with." Spit flew again as Cushman said, "You're a filthy little tramp, as much as lickin' the same spoon as those low-livin' vermin. The way they breed like rats, and you'll be right in there with 'em. It makes me sick to think about it."

Tommy could feel the hatred emanating from the man, along with his raw physical power. Tommy wished he could break free and run, but Cushman's grip, plus the evil eye that the Mexicans thought could give a curse, had him petrified. Even if he could get loose, Cushman could swoop down on him in an instant, and failing that, he could put a bullet in him.

Cushman waved the quirt, and Tommy wondered what he was going to do with it — whether he was going to whip Tommy, or scare away Pete, or do something Tommy could not guess. Cushman slapped the dustcoat again and did not release his grasp on Tommy's shirt.

"It makes me wonder what kind of a low way of life you came from, whether you slept six in a bed and had burlap for blankets. Shit in the corner. I know your type. Steal shoes off a dead man."

Cushman's rant was interrupted by the footfalls of a horse. As Tommy twisted to get a look, he expected to see either Lew Greer or Walt McKinney. He was relieved to recognize the clean features of Fred Berwick, with the addition of a pair of spectacles.

"What's goin' on?"

Cushman snapped. "I caught this one nosin' around."

"Lew and Walt are waiting."

"See anything?"

"Just a Mexican kid on one of their skinny horses. By himself."

"He's with this one. I saw 'em earlier."

Tommy's dislike came to the surface as Cushman relaxed his grip but did not let him go. The man had known what he was up to, or at least who he was with, and he went on to torment Tommy because he had the power to do it.

"We'll go. But first one thing." Cushman glared, shook him by the shirt, and seethed through his yellow teeth. "Now, you listen to me again. If I ever catch you doing anything, on or anywhere near my land, you'll get what your rotten little friend did."

He released his grip and pushed Tommy back.

Tommy stumbled and regained his footing. He exchanged a glance with Fred Berwick. The spectacles were something new, but they looked natural on Fred. Furthermore, they seemed to aid him in giving a neutral expression, as if he was looking out through a window.

"Let's go," said Cushman. With a rustle of his dustcoat, he strode away from Tommy. Twenty yards back, he gathered the reins on a large sorrel horse and turned him around so that the animal stood a few inches downhill. Cushman stuck his boot in the stirrup, grabbed the saddle horn with his two large hands, and swung aboard. He did not look back as the horse trotted away, swishing its tail. The man's dustcoat, with its caped shoulders, looked like the wings of a large, dark bird. *El zopilote.*

Tommy felt empty, as if every bit of energy had been drained from him. He made an effort to steady his wobbly legs as he walked toward his horse. Pete stood with his reins on the ground, waiting and watching. Tommy sensed that the horse understood and sympathized, but even if he didn't, he stood still while Tommy, weak and hollow, needed two attempts to pull himself into the saddle and get seated. His legs were still shaking as he caught his other stirrup and evened his reins.

He rode to higher ground and headed east, in the direction Fred Berwick had come from. After half a mile he saw Gabriel on the brown horse, trying to catch the sand-colored burro with the striped cross. The burro dodged one way and the other, and Gabriel followed. He had a rope, but he never got close enough to drop it over the burro's head and tall ears. On one toss he landed the loop on the animal's nose and forehead, and on another toss he bounced it off the back of the burro's neck.

Tommy untied his rope as Pete trotted down the slope and took them across the dry creek bed. By the time he rode near Gabriel, Tommy had built a loop and was ready to try. Pete knew right away what Tommy wanted, so he cut right when the donkey did, and he cut left when the donkey stutter-stepped on his little hooves and cut back. When the animal was running smooth in one direction, Pete picked up speed and Tommy made his toss. The loop sailed over the tall ears and the tip of the nose and settled around the animal's large neck. Gabriel smiled, and Tommy smiled back as he wrapped the rope around the saddle horn.

Pete stopped and dug in, and the burro jerked to the side. He moved his hind end around and pulled back. Gabriel rode up behind the sand-colored animal and whipped him on the hind end with the loose end of the rope.

"¡Ándale, burro!" he called.

To Tommy's relief, the burro gave in and stepped forward. Tommy and Pete fell into line and headed north. Gabriel rode up on the other side of the donkey and hollered, "¡Ya, ya!" to keep it going.

Tommy let out a slow breath and evened his reins again. He was pleased with himself for making a good toss in front of Gabriel, and he was glad the burro wasn't giving them any more trouble. It could have been a long day with a strong little beast like this one.

Back in camp, the blackish-brown burro with the white nose and belly was tied snug to a wagon wheel. People were picking up the last of their belongings and shoving them into the wagons. The sheep had crossed the creek and now reflected the sunlight a mile to the east. With the arrival of the remaining vagabond burro, activity picked up. Men hitched the horses and burros to the wagons and carts, and the move began.

The Romero brothers crossed the creek first, then Raimundo's wagon, and then Alejo's. Anita, Elsa, and Milena walked alongside the wagons, while Milena's two children rode in the wagon with Raimundo and Eusebia. Gabriel had set off on foot to catch up with the sheepherders.

Tommy sat on his horse and poked along. The whole procession moved at a slow pace, much slower to him now that he was on horseback and not walking. He felt as if he should be doing more, and he felt guilty at seeing the young women on foot while he loafed along in the saddle. For the present, though, he did not know what else to do. As his thoughts wandered, he wished he had told Raimundo about his run-in with Vinch Cushman. Now was not a good time. He would tell him when they made camp again.

They arrived at water in the late afternoon, after they had passed the herd of sheep. Tommy saw at once that their destination was a water hole, a large pool of muddy-looking water with a fifty-yard slope of pocked, drying mud leading to it. The water was no good for human consumption, unless a person strained it two or three times and then boiled it. But it was fit for animals, and it would tide them over until the people found better water the next day. Meanwhile, as each family had a supply of water, the people would get by as well.

As the wagons rolled in and parked in the usual haphazard way, Tommy saw what was on hand for the evening meal. The people killed two pens' worth of chickens and used the wood from the crates for the evening fire. They set up a big pot of water, and by the time the steam was rising off the surface, they had plucked and cleaned and cut up the chickens. Tommy had to look twice to be sure, but he verified that the feet of the chickens went into the pot along with the legs. He grimaced. Prospects improved a little with a cutting board full of diced-up shriveled potatoes, followed by a pound or so of puny white onions, halved and quartered. Milena shook in a dose of salt, then a small wooden spoonful of oregano. A handful of crushed, dried red chile topped it off.

Without much else to do, Tommy observed Milena. He sensed her presence as a full woman, very capable in her tasks and confident in herself. And as Tommy had mentioned to Anita, Milena had pride. She also had an attractive physical presence, and though she was out of Tommy's age range, he appreciated the maturity of a woman who had children and knew how to be a wife to a man. He wondered if that was what Anita would be like in another ten years, and it was not a bad prospect.

Vapors from the big pot floated on the air. They carried the smell of chicken soup, with enough of the other spices to make Tommy's eyes water and his nose burn. As he waited for the evening meal to come around, he remembered to tell Raimundo about his encounter with Vinch Cushman.

Raimundo nodded. "It is a good thing we moved camp. Stay out of his way."

Tommy did not feel so safe. He thought that wherever they went, they would be dogged by Cushman. But it was only a feeling, or a fear, maybe, so he said no more.

The moon was a sliver in the dark sky, but it gave some light. Tommy sat up in his bed, trying to place something that didn't fit. He had been dreaming about working on a ranch, sort of a combination of the White Wings Ranch and the Muleshoe. Either he had heard something in his dream, or a noise from outside had entered his dream. He was used to hearing the sounds of animals in the night, such as the shifting of a horse's hooves, a snuffle, or a cough. Here among the people and wagons he had become accustomed to other noises. The donkeys did not bray when they had company, but they wheezed as a matter of course, and the goats had their soft bleating sound whenever something stirred them. Even the chickens, though there were fewer of them now, clucked at random in the night, and the mutter of sheep came drifting across the distance from the bed ground.

But what he had heard, if only in his dream, was the undertone of cattle. It was not a lowing or a mooing but rather a mixture of *bahs* and grunts that came from a group of the big-bellied creatures. He could picture them lumbering and drooling. Now he heard them again as he sat up in his bedroll — the heaving of breath and the clumsy thud of hooves. The animals were moving.

The footfalls came faster now, drumming. Brush snapped. Then came a man-made sound, a slapping like a glove or the end of a rope on leather chaps. Tommy wanted to yell, but for a few seconds he held himself back, afraid to make a fool of himself with the older men. Then he didn't have to call out anything. The piercing *"Yeah! Yeah! Yeah!"* of a cowpuncher cut into the air, hooves thundered, and people all around him broke out into shrieks and hollers.

A chill ran through him, and his neck and shoulders tightened as he grabbed for his boots and pulled them on. He found his hat and clapped it on his head, then bunched up his bedroll and stuffed it under the wagon along with his saddle. In a matter of seconds he was on his feet and running.

In the moonlight he saw the shapes of Pete and the Villarreals' horse where he had staked them out at sundown. The horses were snorting, twisting around, and pulling on their ropes. Tommy grabbed Pete's rope first. He positioned himself square in front of the horse, dug in his heels, and pulled. The horse settled onto all fours. Tommy remembered driving the stakes deep, and this was no time to be trying to pull them out. He picked and worked at the knot until he had the first rope free. He moved to the second horse, which was wheezing through his nostrils as he pulled and sidestepped and hunched up. For a skinny old horse, the animal had plenty of energy in a moment of danger. Tommy yanked on the stake rope and pushed at the knot until he worked it loose.

The cow hooves rumbled as women screamed and men yelled. A goat cried. Dogs barked. Tommy held onto the brown horse's rope as he turned Pete so as not to get tangled. He grabbed Pete's mane, put the palm of his hand on Pete's back, and boosted himself up so that his chest was on Pete's spine. He climbed around until he was parallel with the horse, then settled into bareback position. Holding the lead rope off to the side, he got a new hold on Pete's mane and touched his heel to the horse's ribs. Pete took off, and the brown horse labored to keep up.

A quarter-mile off, Tommy stopped the horses and turned. The cattle were crashing among the wagons and trampling the area. Wood broke and cracked, metal thumped. A wagon creaked as it settled back onto its wheels. Female voices shrieked, and children cried. A goat was blaring now, and one dog was yapping in retreat.

The cattle thundered north through the camp with riders sticking close and hollering, *"Yip! Yip! Yip! Hee-yeah!"* Tommy guessed the herd at about fifty head, big enough to cut a wide path of destruction but small enough that a handful of riders could keep it together and drive it fast.

Tommy counted five men on horseback, but because of the dust and the turmoil and the thin moonlight, he couldn't be sure of any of them. At least two men and possibly a third had large, hulky figures. Tommy ticked off the White Wings crew that came to mind: Fred Berwick, Walt McKinney, Lew Greer, and Vinch Cushman. Four men, five riders. Then he recalled the two bull-dogs. Fred hadn't mentioned them when he met up with Vinch, but they had probably been on hand. That made sense. None of the riders had the taller, cloaked figure of Cushman, but between Greer and the bulldogs, the hulks were easy to account for.

The hoofbeats receded, as did the *"Yip! Yip!"* of the herders. The stampede had lasted but a few minutes. With the greater noise fading, groans and dull cries were now spreading through the camp. Someone was beating a spoon on a pan. The voices of women rose and fell, and the crying of children was steady. Two men with lanterns were moving around, calling out and get-ting answers.

Tommy took the horses into camp at a walk. Dust hung in the air, as did the linger-ing smell of cattle. Voices ranged from murmuring to wailing. A third lantern had been lit, and men were surveying the dam-age. Tommy stayed back a few yards, but he got a full view.

Blankets were trampled, and eating utensils were scattered. Buckets were tipped over. A metal washtub was crumpled. A wooden water cask had been knocked over and was leaking. A four-legged stool was crushed flat. A chicken coop had been broken open, and chickens wandered in and out of the light.

The brown-and-white goat lay lifeless at the end of its rope. Nobody in the Villarreal family was paying it any attention, though. They were all gathered at the next wagon over. Raimundo held a lantern as Alejo and his wife kneeled on the ground. Anita and her mother were standing close by, holding each other and crying. Milena was holding her two children close to her hips.

Tommy stopped at the edge of the lamplight. The two horses shifted and moved but did not try to pull away. After a few minutes, Gabriel caught sight of Tommy and moved toward him.

Tommy spoke in a low voice. "What happened? Is someone hurt?"

"My cousin Elsa. The cows ran over her."

"Is she hurt bad?"

"I don't know, but I think so. My aunt is praying."

Tommy did not think he could do any good, and he did not want to be in the way. "I have the horses," he said. "I suppose we should look to see if any animals are missing."

"People are looking right now."

"Well, I'll take these out of the way."

For the next few hours until dawn, people searched through the wreckage and picked up their belongings. The cattle had jostled a couple of wagons, but none of them was damaged. Smaller items were broken, like the water cask, wooden buckets, a lantern, plates, and cups. Spoons were ground into the dirt. Aside from the goat, no other animals had been hurt or killed. The only person who had been injured was Elsa.

Through the slow vigil, things did not sound any better for her. Tommy could tell from the people's voices when they joined in prayer and when they appealed to God. He heard the words *Padre, Dios,* and *Señor.* Father, God, and Lord. The people were wearing themselves down with worry and crying. The spirit of the whole group seemed to have sunk to the lowest point just before dawn, and then everything broke. The cries and the sobbing rose, and a wail of sorrow flowed. Voices called in prayer and in pleading. Tommy understood enough of the meaning that he could put it in his own words to himself. *Elsa. May God take you and protect you. Elsa, you are with God.*

CHAPTER TEN

The herd of sheep moved out ahead in the first full sun of morning while the people in camp pulled themselves and their things together. A combined feeling of sorrow, dread, and resentment permeated the camp. Tommy could feel it — empty, heavy, and bitter all at once. Elsa's parents placed her body in the wagon, wrapped in a sheet, to be buried later. They stacked the wooden boxes around her and covered the load with a canvas. Alejo's anger and grief were in full view all the while, and his wife, Leonila, did not cease in her sobbing.

Today the wagons waited so that the group could travel together in a caravan. Every driver's seat had a rifle or a shotgun at hand. Faustino Romero stood next to his wagon in the lead, arms crossed, in a posture of command as if he were the wagon master. With his back to the sun, he made an impressive figure. He wore his straw hat and drab work clothes, and in contrast, he had on display his gunbelt with the silver-inlaid black holsters and the white-handled revolvers jutting out.

Tommy stood by his horse, waiting for the last couple of groups to show that they were ready to go. No one was going to hurry anyone else at a time like this, when violation and mourning hung in the air. Tommy sensed that patience was natural to Raimundo in these circumstances, even when both Romero brothers now stood with their arms folded, waiting.

As for himself, Tommy felt that people ignored him, or perhaps made an effort not to notice him. They all knew he was on their side, but he was still a *gabacho,* a fair-skinned American like the men who had carried out Cushman's act of aggression. And Tommy knew that at least some of the people were convinced that he was part of the reason for Cushman's vendetta. Maybe he was.

Tommy had put on his own gun and holster that morning, not because he thought he would shoot anybody that day but because he felt it was his responsibility to protect, or to do his share in protecting, the people he lived with. He could not imagine himself broad and powerful enough to protect the group, but he could picture himself standing in front of Anita to face the threat. He knew at the same time that it was a fancy idea, almost a schoolboy daydream, and he thought that the pistol on his hip could be seen by others as showing off. So their ignoring him was, in a way, a comfort.

The wagons began to move. Tommy snugged the near rein and mounted up. He moved his horse off to one side, where he waited as the wagons strung out in order. Horses and burros pulled, people walked alongside, goats followed, and dogs ran to and fro. Tommy waited. He had decided to fall in behind like a rear guard.

As the wagons rolled out, they left behind a littered campsite. The wreckage lay strewn where it had been trampled — bits of cloth, the broken wooden cask, the crumpled metal tub, the brown-and-white goat stretched out and beginning to bloat in the morning sunlight. All of the debris lay now on the open range, next to a mudhole that looked like a sore on the landscape.

Tommy shifted his gaze to the wagons ahead. Only Elsa, the treasure, wrapped in a sheet, was being carried away, like a jewel in a rosewood casket.

A familiar feeling haunted him. He recognized it as he rode on in silence. It was the way he had felt about Red's passing — a young person, now gone for no good reason, losing out on all the chances, good and bad, that the rest of life might have held. And yet the two young people were not the same. Deep down, Tommy had always felt there was something flawed about Red. He hadn't felt that way about Elsa, except that she had been friendly to Red, and the attraction hadn't lasted long. Now they were together, in a strange way, though they were drawing farther apart. Elsa was going away. Tommy wondered if Red had in any way been responsible for Elsa dying. He felt that he himself had been, and so he felt guilty twice over — for helping bring Cushman's wrath upon the people, and for going on living when Elsa died.

He swallowed hard as his throat constricted and tears came to his eyes. He made himself think of something better, of the beauty of Elsa when she was alive, and of the bittersweet beauty of her going away, loved and cherished by her family and people.

That was more than Red ever had, and Tommy was sure it was more than he himself would have had if the cattle had trampled him to death. The people would have buried him by the mudhole.

There he was again, thinking of himself, when someone innocent had died and when her family, including Anita, had real grief to suffer. Tommy took in a deep breath, told himself to brace up, and fell into line with the procession.

The wagons did not stop at midday but pushed on to arrive at the next camp in midafternoon. If the group had not been so weighed down by sadness, the site would have had a pleasant atmosphere. A stream flowing from the northwest made a single bow around a grassy area on higher ground. Box elder trees and a few young, bright cottonwoods grew along the bank on the near side. Tommy could see that both the location and the layout were very good. The place had water and a bit of wood, and as the campsite did not lie out in the open, it would be less susceptible to another stampede. In addition, he was glad to see the people place the wagons and carts in a circular arrangement with the camp area in the middle.

With the wagons unhitched and the animals set out to graze, a few people sat and stood around to eat. Some people had eaten along the way, and all of the food consisted of leftovers or other small portions at hand. For his part, Tommy had a cold bowl of soup with a few shreds of chicken meat and some remnants of potato.

As he was finishing his brief meal, he became aware of Raimundo standing at his right. Looking up, he saw the older man's solemn expression.

In a low voice Raimundo said, "We are going to have the burial now."

Tommy nodded. This was a time to say nothing and to let others talk.

"Everybody will go, of course."

Tommy held his breath.

"But it is not good for everybody to turn their back." Raimundo motioned with his hand. "The camp, you know. If we could have someone to look out."

"Oh. Me?"

"If you can. If it can be done."

Tommy blinked. "Sure. Of course." He wondered if he was being excluded, but he told himself it didn't matter. He would treat it as if he was performing a valued service, which might even be the case.

"We give our thanks. Everyone is worried that trouble will come again."

"With good reason." Tommy glanced toward the north end of camp, where people were beginning to gather. He said, "I'm sorry for what happened, and I know I'm not really a part of the rest of the group, but I —" His words escaped him, but others came. "My thoughts will be there."

"Thank you. There will be much praying, for everyone. I am sure some of us will pray for you, too."

"For me?"

"For the young, and the unprotected, and for everyone who is exposed to danger."

"I'm not very good at any of that. Praying, that is. I haven't been to church very much."

"We are all the same in the eyes of God."

"Someone will speak, though? Or read from the Bible?"

"Oh, yes. And later, when things are better, we will come back with a priest. But God does not forget anybody."

Tears came to Tommy's eyes. He wanted to tell Raimundo to tell Elsa he loved her, but he could not think of any way to say it except in the plain words that he could not bring himself to say. Instead he said, "I will keep an eye on everything."

Raimundo nodded and pointed toward his own eye, in a gesture that Tommy had become used to. Then he gave a brief smile of assurance and walked away.

Not everybody came back from the funeral at the same time. Faustino and his brother, Emilio, were among the first. They set up the fire pit while two other men went to the edge of the watercourse to look for firewood. They all continued to ignore Tommy, so he did not offer to help. He minded his own business, standing at the edge of camp and keeping an eye out. Behind him he could hear the people who had not come back from the burial. Their voices rose and fell together in prayer and separately in cries of lamentation.

Gabriel arrived a while later and said they were going to kill a sheep. An old ewe, or mama sheep, as Gabriel put it, that had failed to raise her lamb this last time, was limping after all of the recent walking, and so she was going to provide the next meal. Tommy asked if they needed help, and Gabriel said, no, not in the killing. There were men who always did that, to make sure it was done right. But because Tommy was good at cutting meat from the bone, he could help with the stew.

Tommy agreed and stayed where he was, looking out for trouble that he did not think would come in broad daylight. The afternoon was warm, and the landscape grew hazy in the distance, as voices and crying continued to carry from the site of Elsa's grave.

Steam was drifting from the top of the cauldron, wafting the odor of mutton along with the smell of pepper, red chile, and oregano. Under Milena's hand, everything from the old ewe, including the heart, liver, and kidneys, had gone into the pot. Tommy's hands felt of fat and smelled of mutton, and he was glad of the prospect that all the raw meat was being cooked into a better state.

The sun was setting beyond the low horizon when the stew was ready. With the camp more centralized than before, almost the whole company sat gathered around the campfire area, though back a ways from the heat. Elsa's parents stayed close to their wagon, and a couple of men and one boy were out looking after the sheep, but as nearly as Tommy could tell, everyone else was present. Two women ladled the stew into bowls, and the food was handed out.

Faustino had withdrawn when Milena had been tending the pot, but now that she sat a few yards away with Anita and Eusebia,

Faustino stood in plain view in his oratory posture. He had traded his straw hat for his ornate sombrero, he had put on a short-waisted jacket, and he was wearing his gun-belt with the brace of pistols.

Tommy did not take it as a personal affront when Faustino addressed the group in Spanish. The people spoke that way around him all the time, and he had developed an ability to follow the gist of a conversation even if he could not parse out the words or details to himself in English. Still, he found something disagreeable in Faustino's method, as the man began speaking, with very little preliminary matter, about the young Americans.

This was a sad day, Faustino began, and the troubles were shared by everyone. And yet all of the troubles commenced when the two young Americans began coming around. Nobody could deny that the trouble from the outside came from Americans, from the malice of Cooshmon, the ugly one, and the men who did his work.

Here Faustino paused, with his left hand on a pistol butt and his right hand held out, palm up. He went on. Even though Cooshmon was the aggressive one, and he hated the Mexicans beyond comprehension, yet he also had some kind of vengeance for the young Americans. Killing the first one was not enough, just as cutting off our water and burning our houses was not enough. And so this one, even if he was not the primary cause, should not be ignored. He was bad luck, and he brought bad fortune to the people.

Alejo appeared out of the shadows, short and dark and turbulent. Firelight played on his swollen face and reflected in his bloodshot eyes. Everyone turned to look at him. He raised his head and sniffed as he wiped his eyes. Addressing Faustino and then the rest of the group, he said that Faustino was reasonable in all that he said, but it did not do any good. The person responsible for all the badness, the man who caused the damage and the misery that could not be undone, was the disgraceful Cooshmon. That was where they should place the blame, and that was where they should seek revenge. They should take up, every man among them, all of their rifles and pistols and shotguns, and they should go after Cooshmon. They should kill him, and his foreman El Gordo, and the others who rode with them, including the one who was always neat and clean as well as the one who shot the dog. Alejo's mouth trembled as he went on. If only Cooshmon had been content with killing a burro and a dog and with burning their houses. But he took it further, and the people needed to do something now, not only to get even with what had been done but to prevent this pestilence from visiting them again.

Alejo hung fire after this barrage, and Tommy felt relieved that not all eyes were on him. He thought Faustino would answer, but silence floated in the camp for a moment.

Now Raimundo stood up. As the people turned their attention toward him, Tommy had the sense that Raimundo had more authority, or at least earned more agreement, than either of the other two. To Tommy's surprise, Raimundo spoke in English.

"Alejo, you and I are like brothers. Our wives are sisters. And so the death of your daughter hurts me deeply, also. I believe as you do, that Cooshmon is the guilty one in all of this, and that he should be punished. But I do not think we should run to our guns and horses and try to do it. We all know that God punishes. *Dios castiga.* I believe that if Cooshmon comes again, we should defend ourselves. But I do not believe we should go after him." Raimundo shifted his feet and directed his gaze across the dying fire toward Faustino. "And I do not believe that this boy is at fault. The blame is not his. He has made his contributions to us, *la gente.* The people. He has not caused any trouble in our town, *o bien,* in our camp. Let us agree with my brother-in-law, Alejo, that Cooshmon is the one to blame, and if he comes again, let us show him that we have our pride and we defend ourselves. With lead and steel." Raimundo ended his speech with an upward flourish of his hand.

Faustino remained in his stoic pose, with his arms folded and his face expressionless except for the trace of haughtiness that never disappeared. Although the man did not speak, Tommy had the impression that he was thinking it through and would come back with a renewed argument at some later time.

The sliver of a moon had grown just enough for Tommy to notice, and it cast a glow like the night before. The stars were shining in a clear sky. As Tommy lay in his blankets outside the loose circle of wagons, staring upward, he had a clear sense of where things were in relation to one another. The horses and donkeys and goats were staked out on the grass to the west of camp. On the east side and downslope a ways, the creek ran silent. He had not been able to see it from camp in the evening, and it did not gurgle like a mountain stream flowing over rocks, but he could feel its presence. Clean and clear, a foot deep and a yard wide, it was the best water they had camped on since leaving the village.

The animals had all drunk their fill. The sheep were now bedded down for the night, just south of the higher ground where Tommy lay outside the wagons. He could hear their stray sounds, a scuff here and a mutter there. Two men were on watch. Tommy had heard their voices when he first crawled into his blankets, and though he did not hear anything from them now, he knew the general layout of the camp and so had a mental picture of the two men.

Tommy rolled onto his side and closed his eyes. This was the fourth camp. He understood that the people intended to stay here until they could decide on their next course of action. Someone — Faustino, according to the original plan — was going to try to find a sheriff or a judge who would help restore law. The people were running low on food, so Tommy imagined that Faustino would buy supplies at the same time. He would need to take a couple of pack animals. His brother would probably go with him, then. However it worked, the camp and the group would be left incomplete until Faustino came back. Tommy did not think the man would mind being that important.

A few sounds carried from within the enclosure of wagons — a muffled question and answer in Spanish, an undertone of prayer, the creak of a wagon as someone crawled out, the *woof* of a dog and the low voice of a man.

The *woof* sounded again, higher and louder, followed by the sharp bark of a dog down by the sheep herd. Then came the beat of hooves — not the drumming or rumbling of cattle but the clearer sound of a few horses, loping. One of the men on guard shouted in Spanish. Two dogs were barking below, by the sheep, and the dog in the camp was barking as well. Now both men were running up the hill from the sheep and were hollering at the people in the camp. Voices from within hollered back.

Tommy was wide awake, sitting up straight, his heart pounding as he pulled on his boots and felt around for his hat. They were at it again! Just as he had done the night before, he bunched up his bed, pushed it and his saddle beneath the wagon, and ran toward the place where he had picketed the horses. Halfway across the open ground, he realized he had stowed his pistol and rifle under the wagon with his saddle and the jumble of bedding. His pistol was wrapped in his coat, and the rifle was in the scabbard as always.

The sheep were crying out, raising a terrible chorus of *baa-aah-aah!* Voices in the camp were shouting in Spanish, and voices from below were hollering *"Hee-yah! Hah! Hee-yah!"*

Tommy stopped and turned. They were not stampeding this time. They were rousting the sheep. As he listened, he realized the cries were not of running sheep; they were cries of agony. He heard a faint thud, then another. The men on horses were clubbing the sheep.

Tommy ran back to the wagon and groped among his bedding to find his jacket with the gun wrapped in it. There was no time to buckle on his belt and holster. He pulled the pistol from the bundle and moved in a crouch.

The scene below was murky. In the faint moonlight, three or four horsemen, maybe five, moved among the sheep. Tommy could hear the impact now, thuds and cracks, and he could see the up-and-down motion of arms extended into clubs. The forms were grotesque, and one man was shouting cruel, obscene curses that rose above the clamor of the panicked and dying sheep.

The men on horseback were out of pistol range, and Tommy's heart was beating in his throat. His hand holding the pistol was shaking. He was sure that if he went down the slope by himself and fired, one of the horsemen would run him down and club him, or shoot him in the back. He squatted on his heels, glad he had taken off his spurs that evening. He held the pistol in both hands, trying to steady himself and decide what he should do.

Two men ran past him on the left, one tall and one short. Twenty yards downslope they stopped, and each of them fired a rifle.

The scene changed. The horsemen quit clubbing and shouting and began to ride out from among the sheep. The two men from the camp fired again, and the men on horseback went into faster motion. Two of them took off toward the south, and three others headed toward the camp. Tommy identified Alejo's voice and then Faustino's as belonging to the two men who had fired shots. They stood facing the mass of crying sheep and the men who were emerging from it.

The horsemen rode forward, each on a trot by himself but headed in a common direction toward the two men on foot. Tommy could not pick out the riders, but he thought that two of them, hulking in the moonlight, were the new hired men that Red had referred to as the bulldogs. The third one looked like the slender form of Walt McKinney.

Alejo fired, with no effect except that the riders sped up. The one on the far left rode up to within fifteen yards of Alejo, turned his horse, and fired a pistol. Alejo let out a sharp *"Ayy!"* and fell backwards, dropping his rifle.

Faustino, quite cool, it seemed to Tommy, stood his ground and fired at the bulky horseman. He must have hit him square, for the man let out a grunt like a pole-axed hog and fell forward on his horse's neck.

The other heavy-set rider raced to his side, grabbed his reins, and held him in the saddle as the two horses sped away.

It all happened in a few seconds. Faustino, meanwhile, ejected the spent casing and levered in a new shell. As he was lining up on the jostling pair, the third rider came in from the right and hollered at the other two.

"Look out!"

Tommy was sure it was Walt McKinney's voice, and he was sure it was Walt McKinney's hand that raised a six-gun and pointed it at Faustino, who had flinched and was taking aim again.

Tommy stood up. The rider was some twenty yards away, but it was a long distance in the moonlight. Tommy used both hands to raise his six-gun, and though he tried to hold it steady, he jerked the trigger and fired wide.

McKinney yanked on his reins, cut the horse sharp to the right, and raced away in the wake of his two companions.

Raimundo and another man now appeared alongside Faustino, and each of them threw a rifle shot in the distance.

Faustino said, *"Ya no tiene caso. Están muy lejos,"* which Tommy interpreted as meaning that there was no use in shooting anymore, as the men were too far away. Then Faustino said, *"Creo que le dieron a Alejo."*

Raimundo lowered his rifle and located his brother-in-law lying on the ground. He knelt by Alejo and said, *"No, hombre."* After touching the body, he said, *"Ay, qué terrible. Está muerto."*

Tommy knew the last word for sure. He had heard it a few times by now. It meant *dead.*

■ ■ ■ ■

Cries of dismay and sorrow carried through the night air as Tommy and Gabriel followed Faustino and his brother in surveying the damage. Raimundo had sent the boys to go along, but Faustino and Emilio, each carrying a lantern, ignored them.

The dead and dying sheep were easy to find, as the unharmed sheep had scattered. The searchers counted seventeen dead animals, most of them with their tongues hanging out and blood oozing from their noses and mouths. Another six were dying, three of them lying still and breathing hard, and three of them kicking their legs and choking out gasps. Emilio cut their throats, one by one, as the group came to them and added them to the tally.

Faustino and Emilio spoke to each other in Spanish, but Tommy understood the numbers and followed the meaning. Twenty-three dead sheep left eighty-four to be rounded up in the morning.

Back in camp, the atmosphere was so desolate, the people's spirits so depressed, that no one spoke of fighting or getting even. Nor did they cry out in protest or ask why these things were happening to them.

Tommy did not know what the people thought or if they shared a common opinion. But he did not think they could miss what seemed so evident to him. Cushman was not content with driving the people off their land and burning their houses. He was not content with scaring them and demeaning them, killing their livestock and ruining their remaining property. He hated them more than that. He wanted to crush them all the way.

Tommy was sure the people knew that Cushman's hatred ran deep. But he wondered if they felt, as he did, that Cushman wanted to rub them out, to exterminate them for being what they were.

CHAPTER ELEVEN

The morning sun warmed the air as Tommy
bent over to tie the rope around the sheep's
legs. This was the seventh animal he worked
on. The dead sheep had begun to bloat, and
the dead smell mixed with the odor of warm
wool. Faustino and Emilio had skinned and
gutted two yearlings, as much meat as the
group was likely to eat before it spoiled.
They had finished by daybreak. When the
sun came up, Faustino told Gabriel that he
and his friend should drag the rest of the
dead ones a good ways from camp. Faustino said nothing about a horse, and Tommy
imagined Faustino might have thought he
was putting the boys to work at the miserable job of dragging all the carcasses by
hand. So Tommy was glad he thought of
Pete right away. As Pete had dragged a great
many calves in his time, Tommy did not
hesitate. The horse shied at the smell to
begin with, but he was always a good horse

with Tommy, and he submitted to the task.

With the horse, Tommy was able to drag the dead sheep a quarter of a mile each time, twice as far as he and Gabriel would have dragged them by hand. Gabriel waited behind while Tommy rode, so Gabriel spent most of his time loitering by the dead sheep. Even then, Tommy dismounted each time to tie on to the carcass.

Tommy pulled on the rope to make sure the loop was snug on the two ankles. He held out the slack and walked along the rope, then pushed at Pete to move him around so that the rope would not be in the way when he mounted up. He stepped around the horse, keeping his hand on Pete's rump for assurance. On the other side, he grabbed the reins and saddle horn, poked his toe in the stirrup, and swung aboard. When he was seated, he gave Pete the go-ahead. The rope tightened against Tommy's right thigh, and the dead animal skidded along the dirt and grass and sagebrush.

At the end of the drag, Tommy dismounted and held Pete by the reins as he untied the rope from the sheep's ankles and coiled it up. Back in the saddle, he sat up straight and took a full breath. Seven down, fourteen to go.

As he rode back to the spot where Gabriel stood among the dead sheep, he saw that Gabriel was holding something level in front of his waist. Closer, he saw that it was dark and narrow; closer still, he recognized it as a heavy stick. He drew rein a couple of yards from his friend and swung down. Gabriel held the stick up, as if it were on a platter.

The club was a little more than a yard long. Nearly two inches in diameter, it looked like a thick piece of chokecherry, with dark, skin-like bark. The grip had been whittled clean, with nicks of lighter color showing against the reddish tan of the under layer. The last half-inch of the handle had been left at full thickness, to keep the hand from slipping off, and a looped leather thong was tied snug against the inside of that wider ridge or knob. This wasn't just a stick picked up at random; somebody had taken time to prepare for the attack.

Tommy said, "I bet they wished they hadn't left that here. But if it belonged to the one Faustino shot, it's probably the least of his worries." Tommy looked in the direction where the marauders had galloped away in the night. "I know we're not supposed to think this way, but I hope he's dead." Tommy's eyes burned. "Even if he is, and even if Faustino had shot two or three more, it wouldn't bring back Elsa or your uncle. I'm sorry."

"I hate them, too," said Gabriel.

"You have a right to." Tommy pictured Gabriel's own sister and father. "Everyone does. Everyone has a family." He realized he meant everyone but himself, but he thought he had said enough. Nodding at the club, he said, "What do you call that in Spanish?"

Gabriel shrugged. *"Un palo. Un bastón. Más bien una porra."* He dragged out the last word with its double *r* and repeated it. *"Una porra."*

"Something to keep."

"Oh, yes. You have your pistol, and now I have this."

Tommy sat in the shade of the wagon at a little after midday, the customary mealtime with the people. He reached up and accepted the bowl of stew that Milena handed him. *"Gracias,"* he said.

"De nada. Provecho." You're welcome. Enjoy the meal.

His spirits lifted as he took in the promising smell of the food. After the morning's work, he had washed his hands and face in the creek and had tried to clear the smell of dead sheep from his nostrils. The steam and

229

the spices from the stew were making an improvement. It was the last of the big pot from the evening before. He had enjoyed it then, and he was hungrier now. He took a spoonful and blew across it. He wanted to make sure he didn't burn his tongue.

He finished the first bowl and was glad to see there was a little more for a second helping. A mournful air hung around the camp, and with good reason, but life went on.

Raimundo put his hand on Tommy's shoulder. "You get enough to eat?"

"Just right. I'm fine, thanks."

"That's good. You gotta eat. Everything else goes to hell, you gotta eat." Raimundo patted him again. "That's good work you do this morning. Even that far away, maybe we'll still get the smell."

"Depends on which way the wind blows."

"That's right. But there's a lot of dead ones."

"I'm sorry it happened. All of it."

Raimundo shrugged. "Nothin' we can do about it. Just try to help Leonila. This is all too heavy for her."

"Do you think Cushman's men will come again?"

"Sooner or later. He doesn't give up. He wants to punish us too much."

"Well, I'll help if I can."

"I know. You're a good boy." Raimundo patted him one more time. "Faustino doesn't want to say anything good about you, but everyone knows you helped. When you fired your pistol."

"I didn't hit anything."

"I know. But you helped."

Tommy handed in his empty bowl and looked for another place to sit. The shade had moved, and now he found a place between the wagons where he could rest for a while and gaze out to the south. The sun beat down on a warm, calm, dry afternoon. The bed ground where the attack had taken place looked bare and innocent now. The blood and the dug-up dirt were not visible at this distance.

Tommy had gotten comfortable in the shade when movement at the right edge of his vision caught his attention. A half-mile to the southwest, a lone rider was making his way in the direction of the camp. Tommy's heartbeat picked up, and he felt to make sure his pistol was in place. Pete was staked out and cropping grass a quarter of a mile to the west. Tommy narrowed his eyes but could not make out the rider any better. He made himself wait. If he didn't like the looks of the man or anything about him, he would go for his horse and be ready.

A few minutes passed, and the horse and rider continued in their own shadow. Another minute went by, and the horse did not look as dark. The rider's outline became clearer. He was not a large man. Tommy doubted that one of Cushman's men would come back by himself, either to repay a debt or to fetch a club. Still, no rider was a friend unless — and Tommy's thought began to be confirmed. The horse had a flecked grey coat and dark ears. The rider wore a dusty black hat. For a few seconds, only the hat showed as the horse went into a low spot. As the form rose up and the pair emerged into closer view, a smile came to Tommy's face, and he waved at Bill Lockwood.

The lean rider waved back, a flash of buckskin-colored glove against the background of his dark shirt. Lockwood's mustache was visible now, and even his posture in the saddle was unmistakable. A hundred yards out, he slowed the grey horse to a walk. The animal was sweating along the neck and breathing hard, its feet still picking up in brisk movements.

"What, ho?" said Lockwood as he brought the horse to a stop and leaned forward with both hands on the saddle horn.

"Good afternoon. What brings you here?"

"An ill wind."

"Really?"

"That's right. Is Raimundo here?"

"Yes, he is."

"Good." Lockwood's coffee-colored eyes looked past Tommy. "There you are. Raimundo. I'm glad to see you." Lockwood dismounted in the slow, deliberate manner of a man who had ridden a long ways. His eyes came back to Tommy. "I can tell you both at the same time."

Tommy observed Raimundo on his left. He heard movement behind him, but he did not turn to see who was on the other side of the wagon. There were no secrets in this camp anyway, at least that he knew of, and anyone could listen.

"Oh?" said Raimundo. "Something bad?"

"Lies, I imagine." Lockwood held the reins behind him as he stepped forward. "One of Cushman's men rode into Fenton this morning and said the Mexicans had attacked their camp and shot one of the men. They didn't expect him to live."

"Which one said it?" asked Tommy.

"That big one they call Lew Greer."

"He's the foreman," Tommy said.

"I think I heard that. Anyway, he didn't seem to have any purpose except to spread the gossip. There's no lawman in that town, and no doctor."

"Well it's a big lie," said Raimundo. "They attack us two times. The first time, they run cattle through our camp, and they kill one person. My niece, Elsa."

Lockwood's face fell.

"The next time, last night, they come and kill our sheep."

Lockwood frowned. "Did they shoot 'em?"

Tommy spoke up. "They clubbed the sheep. They killed twenty-three head, and when the Mexicans started shooting at 'em, they rode up and shot Alejo, Elsa's father. Faustino got a shot at the man who did it, so that would be the one that Lew Greer was talking about."

"Son of a bitch," said Lockwood. "What about Alejo?"

Raimundo answered. "He's dead."

Lockwood shook his head. "And they came to club the sheep, did they?"

"That's right," said Tommy. "I counted five of them. They can deny it, but we've got plenty of witnesses, and one of them left his club behind." Tommy pointed to the south. "And just in case someone still doesn't believe it, they can go look at all the dead ones we had to drag away."

Lockwood let out a low whistle. "That's sure a whole different story. I didn't believe what I heard, but I had no idea it was this bad." He poked his cheek out with his tongue. "This fella's rotten. Not that I ever thought he was any good, but he's gone way out of his way, and to do something like this." He raised his eyes. "Raimundo, I came here to tell you what someone was sayin' about your people, and I thought I'd offer my help if you need it. You can decide."

"You come a long ways. You better get something to eat."

Lockwood took off his gloves, shook them, and tucked them under his gunbelt. He smiled and said, "Sounds good to me."

Raimundo turned and spoke to Tommy. "You take care of his horse, eh? Then you come back and sit with us."

Tommy unsaddled the grey horse and set him out to graze near Pete. Then he stowed Lockwood's saddle, blankets, bedroll, and duffel bag under the wagon, next to his own.

Inside the camp, Lockwood was seated on a wooden box with his hands on his knees, holding his back up straight. Raimundo sat on a box near him. Without saying anything, Tommy took a seat on the ground.

Raimundo was telling Lockwood about the goat he had lost at the previous camp. "He was a good goat. Big one. Brown and white, maybe you remember him. I was gonna make him a leader. You know, he leads the sheep."

"Oh, yeah. I've seen that. They'll lead the sheep right into the slaughterhouse."

"Hah-hah. Yeah, they do that, too."

"They call 'em a Judas goat."

"What kinda goat?"

"A Judas goat. For Judas, the disciple who betrayed Christ."

"Oh, yeah, yeah. That one." Raimundo shook his head. "Well, I was gonna have him lead the sheep when we move 'em. But I didn't have time on this trip. Everything in a hurry."

Milena appeared with a plate of meat in red chile sauce. From the aroma, Tommy guessed it was lamb, the first of the fresh meat from that morning.

Lockwood took the plate and gave Milena a full look of appreciation. He smiled and said, *"Gracias."*

"De nada. Provecho." Then with a smile she produced a spoon from her apron and handed it to him. *"No hay tortillas,"* she said.

"Está bien." He gave her another smile, and his glance lingered as she walked away.

Raimundo did not speak as Lockwood put away the food. Smoke drifted from the cookfire, and a frying pan sizzled.

"Here's what I think," said Lockwood. He

moved some small chunks of meat together on his plate. "I think Cushman and his men will go back and lick their wounds, but I don't believe they're done. They come all this way to torment you, and it looks as if his men have orders to shoot. I expect they'll be back."

"I think so, too. He hates us too much. Like I say to Tommy. But we don't ever do anything to him. He just hates us because we're Mexican."

Lockwood continued to eat as he talked. "I think that's it. He comes from that part of the country where they used to have slaves. Some of those people hate black people, Indians, Mexicans, anyone who's not white. You know they've got laws in some of those states that make it illegal for people of different races to marry each other."

"¡Válgame! And these same people, they have a white cat and a black cat, or a white horse and a brown one."

"That's right. And they think nothin' of it. But when it comes to people, it makes their blood boil. They can't stand it. None of their business what goes on in another man's house, but they want to have a law against it. They'll hang a black man for lookin' at a white woman. You know that."

"Oh, yeah. I heard that. But they do it with a black woman if they get a chance."

"Some. But they still hate the idea so much, they have a law against it."

"They must be afraid of something."

"That's just it. They're afraid of the thing itself. And that's why they hate it."

"*¿Más?*" Milena had appeared to ask if he wanted more.

"*Sí, por favor.*"

Tommy was amused, as he had been on an earlier occasion, by Lockwood's quaint pronunciation.

Lockwood resumed speaking in English. "I think he hates any idea of anyone who isn't white, doing it, like you say, with anyone else."

"Well, he's crazy. There's a lotta people on this earth. They all got a right to have a family."

"Of course there is, but he can't see that far. All he can see is his own world around him. And he hates everything that isn't like him. And you know what else I think? I think he hates it because deep down, he's afraid it *is* like him."

Raimundo sat straight up as he took in a breath. "Well, I say he's crazy."

"You bet he is. He's sick as a poisoned dog. But that's what we're up against. *Gra-*

cias." Lockwood smiled at Milena as she handed him his refilled plate.

"*De nada.*"

Lockwood's eyes lingered again for a few seconds until he returned to his plate. "This is good grub," he said to Raimundo. "*¿Borrego?*"

"Yeah, it's lamb. From the ones they killed. We get something out of it."

No one spoke as Lockwood finished his second helping. He set his plate on the grass and took out his sack of cigarette makin's. He shook tobacco into a paper for himself and passed the bag to Raimundo.

At that point Gabriel joined the group, but before he could sit down, his father spoke to him in Spanish. He left, but he came back in a couple of minutes with a bottle and two small glasses.

"*Una copita,*" said Raimundo as he took the first puff on his new cigarette.

"*Muy bien.*" Lockwood blew away a cloud of smoke.

The afternoon mellowed out, with no further talk of bloodshed or hatred, as the men stayed close to the shade and sipped from their glasses. Tommy and Gabriel sat by and kept quiet as the men chatted in a mixture of Spanish and English.

The sand-colored burro with the striped

cross wandered in, and Lockwood rubbed him on the nose and patted him on the forehead. Milena handed Lockwood half of a scorched corn tortilla. He held it out, and the burro took it and shattered it with his teeth. Fragments fell on Lockwood's shirt, and he brushed it off. Everyone smiled, and the atmosphere felt so relaxed that Tommy felt as if he had had a shot of tequila himself.

When Raimundo drained the last drops into the two glasses, he capped the bottle and tossed it on the grass.

"Another dead soldier," said Lockwood. "The empty bottle."

"Oh, yeah."

The sound of footsteps caused everyone to look up. Faustino Romero, wearing his straw hat and his two-gun outfit, stood with his chin lifted.

Raimundo spoke in English. "Our friend has come back to help us."

"I can see that." Faustino cast a glance at the empty bottle. "Who knows if he brings trouble with him."

"He came to help. And to tell us what Cooshmon is saying about us. Cooshmon, the big liar, says we attacked his camp."

"I have already heard that. Who cares what lies they tell? But here is the thing. No one wants to listen to me. I wanted to leave from the beginning. Everyone said no, and we had to leave anyway. And we had none of this trouble until the two young Americans came. Since then, Cooshmon has done one thing after another to punish us. I believe this one is to blame." He pointed at Tommy. "And who knows what will happen now, with this other one here?" He waved at Lockwood with the back of his hand.

Lockwood stood up, set his hat back on his head, and rested his hands on his hips. "You've got it all backwards, friend. You've got the cart before the horse." Faustino gave a blank expression, so Lockwood said, "You're gettin' the causes and the results all twisted up. This fellow Cushman had it in for all of you before these boys ever showed up. If he has a reason to pick on this boy, it's because he associates with you people, not the other way around. Same with me. He doesn't have a thing against me, or at least he won't until he finds out I've come over to your side."

Faustino had regained his superior pose. "How do you know what he thinks? Is he a friend of yours?"

"I know his mind, and I know his kind. He's vicious, and he's dead wrong. He wants to tell other people how to live and where, what they may or may not do. He's got an old and ignorant way of thinking. This is the Age of Steel, not the Stone Age, but he won't give up. You people have rights, and he doesn't want you to."

Faustino sneered. "Who are you to tell us about ourselves? You're an outsider. You're not Mexican. We don't know who you are or what you are."

"I don't think I've hidden anything. My name's Bill Lockwood, as these people know, and I'm a typical American white man, as anyone can see. A *gringo,* to use your language."

Faustino laughed. "A man is a *gringo* when he's in Mexico. Over here, he's a *gabacho,* an American in his own country."

"Then I guess that's what I am."

"Very good," said Faustino, dragging out the second word. "Then what do you come here for? Are you like these others, another *coyote* in the chicken house, that you just want a girl?"

Now Lockwood laughed. "If there's a girl in it for me, I'm yet to know about it."

"Then why did you come?"

Lockwood patted the six-gun that rode in the holster on his hip. "I came to help. With this, if necessary. Now, if you want to keep crowin' like a rooster, you can tell me you don't need my help." He nodded at Faustino's matched pistols. "Maybe you can do it all yourself, and win a girl that way."

Faustino blanched, and then the color came back into his face with no expression.

Raimundo spoke. "Look, Faustino. I know this gets you in the liver, but leave him alone. You and your brother are going to leave. If this man is here, we have one more gun. You be crazy to run him off."

Tommy found it incongruous, and a little humorous, to hear the men speaking to each other in English, but the atmosphere was serious. Faustino's face remained impassive. As the man turned away, Tommy imagined, as before, that he would come back later with an answer.

A couple of men and a couple of women had formed a small audience on opposite sides of the little theater, and they now dispersed. Milena moved in and picked up the empty bottle. As she stood up, she smiled at Raimundo and said, *"Ay, cómo quedó con el ojo cuadrado."* After a small laugh, she shared her smile with Lockwood and walked away.

Tommy suppressed a smile as he asked Gabriel, "What did she say?"

"She says Faustino stood there with his eye like a square." Gabriel was almost laughing as he held his thumb and forefinger up by his eye, making a square shape.

"I'm sure he's mad."

"Oh, yes. But he knows my father is right."

Tommy thought, *Lockwood is, too,* but he left it at that. And now that he considered it, even Faustino had some grounds, or at least authority, for an argument. When the fight was on, he had stood up and taken his shots.

Movement around camp was slow and quiet when Tommy woke up from a short nap. He gathered his senses as he took in his surroundings. It was late afternoon. Faustino and Emilio had left earlier with two packhorses, and three men and a boy had been out tending sheep. Raimundo and Lockwood had each stretched out for a nap before Tommy did, and they were still snoozing. Voices came from Alejo's wagon, where it sounded as if Eusebia was trying to console her sister. Milena was sitting on a canvas tarpaulin with her two children and was combing the little girl's hair. Anita came around from in back of her family's wagon with two empty buckets and was headed toward the creek.

Tommy stood up and put on his hat. He brushed off the front of his shirt, stepped forward, and intercepted Anita at the edge of the camp. Nervous at the risk of being turned down, he said, "I'll be glad to carry the buckets for you."

"That's all right. I can do it."

"I meant when they're full."

She smiled. "You don't have to."

"Well, I'd like to. Unless you don't want me to help. I don't want to —"

"You can help," she said.

They walked together for a minute without saying anything until he spoke. "I haven't had a chance to tell you, but I'm sorry for what has happened. I know it's very hard for your family. First Elsa, then her father."

Anita kept looking ahead as she said, "Yes, it is sad. Very sad. Elsa was like a sister to me, as I told you before. Our families are very close."

"I feel as if there's something I should do, but I don't know what."

"I don't think there's anything you can do. No one can change what has happened."

"I know. But I still feel guilty, or responsible, or, I don't know. Not helpless, but . . . inadequate. I guess that's a word for it."

"I don't know if you should feel inadequate," she said, swinging a bucket about a foot in front of her. "But there's nothing to feel guilty about. You didn't cause anything.

And my father says you even helped. You might have kept one of the men from shooting Faustino."

"I can't say how much I did, but I tried."

"You won't get a word of thanks from Faustino. To the contrary, he tries to put the blame on you. We can see it. Don't take it to heart, as we say."

Tommy could feel his heart beating, but not for anything Faustino might have said. "Thanks for saying that. All of it. It makes me feel better. There just hasn't been much to feel good about."

"It has been hard for everyone."

The air became cooler as they walked down the hill to the water. The stream had a faint lapping sound and no more.

"Here," he said. "I'll fill the buckets. You've done all the work of carrying them down here."

She smiled and handed him one bucket.

He held the handle and the rim together as he pushed the bottom of the bucket into the current and faced the mouth of it downstream.

"Why do you put it in backwards?" she asked. "You don't get any more, do you?"

He pulled the dripping bucket up out of the water. "No, you get the same amount either way," he said, "and just as fast. But if there's anything floating on the surface, little bits of junk or anything, you're less likely to get it in the bucket."

"I didn't know that."

"I learned it. Someone told me, and I experimented. It seems to be true." He handed her the full bucket and took the empty. When he had the second one filled the same way, he faced her and motioned with his free hand. "Let me take it. It's easier to carry two. Better balance."

She held onto her bucket as he laid his hand on the bail handle.

"Let me have it," he said. He felt her hand against his. It was the first time he had ever touched her, and she was not moving away. He smiled as he drew half a step closer and brought the other bucket near her. "Maybe I should let you hold this one, too." She put her free hand next to his on the handle. He was facing her, very close. Their bodies were almost touching. He saw her close her eyes as he closed his and moved toward her. She was the first girl he ever kissed. Everything around him swirled in near silence, with only the sound of lapping water and the perfect breathing of a beautiful girl.

Chapter Twelve

Tommy ran the brush down the side of Pete's neck and across his withers. He held his left hand against the horse as he worked the brush with his right. The horse's coat was warm and shiny in the early afternoon sun, and the animal stood still. Sounds drifted from the camp. After a somber beginning to the day with Alejo's burial, life had picked up little by little. Tommy heard the bang of a pot, the voice of a woman, and the chattering noise of children as they ran in and out of the enclosure of wagons.

Tommy kept an eye on camp, wishing Anita would walk out into the sunlight and wave to him, or better yet, walk across the open distance and visit with him. But it was only a wish. He knew that Anita and her mother were sitting with Leonila and trying to console her for the loss of her daughter and her husband. He knew he would see Anita again, and he knew he should be patient, but she was all he could think of. His yearning to see her ran through his whole being. Vinch Cushman could have come up behind him and swatted him on the side of the head, and he wouldn't know it until he felt the blow.

He turned to look behind him, to see if the big looming figure was there, but instead he saw a party of men and horses. His pulse jumped and then settled as he recognized Faustino Romero on his bay horse with the white blaze and four white socks. On the other side of the party, Emilio rode his brother's white horse. Each of the Romero brothers led a packhorse with canvas bundles lashed with diamond hitches on top of the panniers.

In the middle of the group, on a horse that was neck and shoulders behind the other two, rode a stranger. He wore a shiny, black leather vest and a black, flat-crowned hat. He had a slender build and rode with something of a slouch. From the configuration, he could have been a prisoner of the Romero brothers, or they could have been his bodyguards. But from the way the Romeros carried themselves, and the way they held their reins and handled their lead ropes, Tommy inferred that the stranger was not in custody but had no special authority, either.

The party rode forward, up the slope, and stopped at the opening where the camp looked out toward the creek. Voices and commotion sounded from within the enclosure, and the children quieted down as they stood between two wagons and looked on.

Tommy continued to brush his horse. He didn't like to join the crowd, and he didn't like to gawk. The Mexicans were not so reserved, though. Tommy had noticed the tendency on other occasions, from the public debates that Faustino liked to stage to the club that Gabriel brought in from the field. Now with the arrival of men and horses, supplies from town, and a stranger in their midst, they had something to look at.

Tommy put his shoulder under Pete's neck and laid his head against the horse as he patted him. He felt alone, knowing that everyone in the camp, including Anita, would be drawn together by the new arrival. But he would go to the camp soon enough. There was nowhere else to go on this little spot in the middle of open country.

By the time he arrived at the wagons and paused at the outside looking in, the Romero brothers had unloaded the top packs and most of the contents of the panniers. The side bags hung open, and the ropes draped onto the ground. Raimundo and Lockwood held the two packhorses while the brothers lifted out canned goods and cotton sacks. As Faustino gave orders, Gabriel and another boy set the provisions on a canvas sheet spread out on the other side of camp. The boys walked back and forth in front of the stranger, who was sitting on a chair.

In addition to his black hat and vest, the man wore a greyish-white cotton shirt, grey wool pants, and black boots. He also wore a gunbelt, with the tip of the holster hanging free and the ivory-handled revolver in plain view. The man had his hand resting on his knee, where smoke curled up from a thin cigarette. Between his feet on the ground, a whiskey bottle stood with a cork sticking out of the neck.

Tommy studied the man's face, less in shadow now than before. The stranger had dark, beady eyes and a clipped mustache. His complexion was shiny and sallow, and his hair lay in oily, wavy strands along his ears and neck. He raised his cigarette, and as he took a drag, his beady eyes peered through the smoke and made Tommy's pulse jump. Something about the man seemed familiar, but Tommy could not place him. The sensation was like that of seeing a snake; a person knew what it was before he made a full identification.

Gabriel walked past with a sack of flour, and the man's eyes shifted. Tommy looked around for Anita, but he did not see her. At that moment, Milena appeared from behind the Villarreals' wagon and spoke to Gabriel in Spanish.

The stranger turned, and his eyebrows went up as he took another drag and gave Milena a look of appraisal. Her eyes went hard as flint, then relaxed as they moved toward Lockwood, glancing over his shoulder. The stranger lowered his head, tapped his ash on the ground, and took a slow look at the American. Lockwood had his back turned again, so the stranger settled into himself, hiked one leg over another, and took a casual drag on his thin cigarette.

Gabriel made a short whistling sound. Tommy thought it was for the other boy, and then he realized it was for him. He came out of his daze as he saw Gabriel beckoning, pawing downward at the air in the way the Mexicans did when they wanted someone to come toward them.

"What do you need?" Tommy asked.

"Milena wants you to cut meat."

"Oh. All right." As Tommy walked toward the far end of the Villarreals' wagon, he felt the stranger's eyes on him.

Milena had a cutting board set out on the tailgate of the wagon, and the remains of a lamb carcass lay next to it on a bloody sheet. Tommy picked up a wooden-handled knife, pointed at the meat, and made a questioning expression.

"Sí. Cortar la carne."

He remembered that he had been working with his horse, so he set down the knife. He rubbed his hands together and said, *"Agua."*

Milena pointed at a bucket of water underneath the corner of the tailgate.

"Bien." He picked up the bucket and carried it a few yards from the wagon. There he splashed out enough water to rinse his hands. He carried the bucket back to the wagon, found a clean spot on the red-and-white sheet, and dried his hands.

The carcass was lying on its side, and the hindquarters were gone. He lifted the front foreleg and cut the shoulder away from the rest of the body. As he laid the piece on the cutting board and was deciding where to begin, he became aware of Anita at his left elbow.

"Well, hello," he said. "How are you?"

"I'm all right. It looks like they have work

for you."

"It's better that way."

"Oh?"

"Sure. This is the first time I've seen you all day."

"Oh, you." She pursed her lips.

"Be careful. You'll make me cut myself."

"You be careful. Maybe I should leave."

"Oh, no, no. Stay here and make sure I do a good job."

"You do well. That's why they give you this work."

"I see." He began to separate the light-colored meat from the shoulder blade. To keep Anita from leaving, he said, "Looks like we've got someone new in camp. Do you know him?"

"We saw him before. When we lived in our houses. He passed by a couple of times."

"What's his name?"

"Alfredo Ortiz."

"He looks like someone they brought in for protection."

"Yes, he does, doesn't he?"

"I thought Faustino was going to go for a sheriff or somebody."

"He says he did, but they have to send for somebody. It may be a week or more."

"Ah-hah. So they bring in a hired gun in the meanwhile. I wonder what your father thinks of him."

"He is not one of us. My father told us before just to stay away from him."

Tommy widened his eyes and repositioned the shoulder he was trimming. "I think that's good advice."

For as much as Tommy preferred to stay clear of Ortiz, he could not very well take his plate and walk away from the camp to eat his supper. So he sat in the company of Gabriel, Lockwood, and Raimundo on their side of the camp, while the Romero brothers, two men who came in from the sheep, and Alfredo Ortiz sat on the other. As was the custom, the men ate first, and the women served the food. Milena served the side of camp where Tommy sat, and she ignored the other side. Eusebia brought plates to the other side, all with a minimum of conversation. *Gracias. De nada. Provecho.*

Anita did not appear. Tommy had noticed that she kept her distance from Faustino in general, and now with the presence of Ortiz, Tommy was not surprised that she did not come into view at all.

The meal consisted of lamb meat cut up small and fried with potatoes and onions. Tommy appreciated the variety, thanks to the new supplies. Even though he knew

255

Faustino resented him, and even though Faustino had brought the snake-eyed Ortiz into the company, Tommy acknowledged the competence of the Romero brothers and their efforts on behalf of the group. Faustino put away his food with authority, and Emilio ate with similar repose, though he seemed to make it an exercise as he lifted his elbow and flexed his muscle. Tommy wondered how much of the show was for the stranger's benefit.

All the men except Ortiz cleaned their plates. The newcomer set his plate with the half-eaten portion on the ground and leaned back to roll himself another thin cigarette. He kept the whiskey bottle between his feet, and Tommy could not see that the level had yet gone down in it. One of the remaining chickens came near. Ortiz kicked at it as he dug out a match, then lit his cigarette.

Faustino set his empty plate on the ground and rose to his feet. He held his head up and looked around, taking in a slow breath. When he saw that everyone was finished eating, he began.

"I believe it is time that we talk again." He nodded in Ortiz's direction. "We all speak in an open manner here. Nobody has to hide what he thinks. I do not talk behind someone's back. I do not throw a rock and hide my hand." He made a slow turn to take in the whole group. "All of you know that." After a pause of a couple of seconds, he continued. "But here is the thing. It is not new. As I said before, I believe that these people are part of our trouble." He made a short wave with his hand. "It began with the two boys. Then the red-haired one, may he rest in peace, went looking for trouble. To be supposed that he did it in our interest, but he only made things worse."

Ortiz sat up and took a hard look at Tommy.

"And now this one," said Faustino, motioning toward Lockwood. "And in the end, with what motive does he stay with us? Like the young one. I think you can see it. In the form of the feminine persons."

"Look here," said Lockwood, standing up.

"Sit down."

"I thought you said everyone gets to speak."

"Each one in his turn. I believe *el señor Ortiz* has something to say."

Lockwood sat down as all eyes turned toward Ortiz. The man did not stand up, but rather held his cigarette between thumb and forefinger and blew a stream of smoke out of the side of his mouth. "Yes," he said. "If it can be permitted, I would like to say something." His English was clearer than Faustino's, and he spoke with a confident air. "This is not my affair, but I believe Mr. Romero is right and just in what he says. For my own part, I have seen this young boy, in the company of his red-haired friend. They were selling a heifer to a railroad crew. A young female cow. The animal had no brand, and the boys took no bill of sale. It was obvious to everyone there."

Tommy felt a prickly sensation spread through his face, neck, and shoulders. His mouth was sealed shut. In his dizziness, the scene began to swim. He made himself bear down and hang on.

Ortiz widened his nostrils and took a slow breath. He didn't seem to mind drawing out the moment until he spoke again. "Maybe it is a small thing, and maybe they did it only once. But it is the type of thing that does not set well with a rancher. Perhaps for that reason he would like to punish this boy." Ortiz hiked his boot onto his knee, squinted his eyes, and took another drag. "That is all I have to say. Maybe the rancher has reasons to come after this boy. Anything else, I don't know."

Faustino tipped his head and widened his eyes, in a taunting expression. He said to

Tommy, "And you? I think it's your turn to speak."

Tommy's mouth was dry, and he could feel himself shaking as he stood up. "The story is true," he said. "I'm sorry I did it. I can't blame it on Red, though it was his idea and I wouldn't have done it by myself. And once I did, it was never worth the small amount of money I made on it." He tried to steady his voice. "But it's in the past. I've decided over and over again that I'm done with that sort of thing."

Faustino laughed. He surveyed the audience, which had grown now with women and children, and he came back to Tommy. "How far in the past can it be? From the looks of you, you still have your baby teeth."

A ripple of laughter went through the other side of camp, and Tommy almost cried. He was trying to form an answer when Faustino spoke again.

His tone was serious now. "I go back to what I said before. These people are trouble. They make things worse. We don't need them." With a nod toward Ortiz he said, "We have all the help we need. It would be better if our American friends would leave."

Lockwood rose again and said, "Very well. We don't want to stay where we're not

259

wanted. No one owes anyone anything. We'll leave."

Silence fell on the group. Tommy stood by himself, feeling alone and humiliated. He couldn't even speak for himself. He could see that Faustino had everything stacked against him, and now with Lockwood speaking for the two of them, he didn't have much choice.

Lockwood, with a nonchalant air, walked toward the back of the camp and out between the Villarreal wagon and the next one. The women and children dispersed, and Milena followed in the direction where Lockwood had gone.

Tommy clenched his teeth and tried to moisten the inside of his mouth. Faustino had shamed him but good, and Ortiz — well, there was no need blaming others, even if they magnified the truth. Tommy took in a breath and tried to build himself back up. He needed to take it like a man and walk out of here with a calm face.

He went the same way Lockwood did. He felt people's eyes on him, as if he was walking through town on the way to jail. He needed to get past the wagons, out where he could gather his horse and his gear and try to pull himself together.

Out in the open, with dusk falling, he saw

Lockwood in a subdued conversation with Milena. He could hear Lockwood's imperfect Spanish. Good for him. Though he had jumped right up and volunteered for both of them to leave, at least he had someone who was sorry to see him go.

Tommy went around the outside of the wagon to look for his saddle, and he almost ran into Anita.

"You're going away," she said.

"I don't have much choice, thanks to Bill Lockwood." He collected himself. "It's not his fault." He met her eyes, and he could tell she felt sorry for him. "I suppose you heard everything they said."

"Yes, and what you said, too."

"Then you know what they're making me out to be. But I can't deny it. I did that one thing. One time. It was the thing I told you about, the day you brought the goats down to the water."

"I know. You said you didn't want to do anything like that again. I believed you."

"And do you believe me now?"

"Oh, yes. I believe you. It's in the past. You're not with Red now."

"I don't want to blame it on him, especially since he's not even here anymore, but I wouldn't have done it by myself."

"I know."

"It's bad enough that someone has to dredge it up from the past, but when that person is as slimy as — well, there I go again, blaming it on someone else."

She touched her fingers to his lips. "Forget it. Everything passes. This man won't be here forever."

"Yes, but what he said will be."

"And what you said, too. You accepted the blame, and you said you are sorry. You didn't try to lie. You know, many people do. They lie with all of their teeth, as we say."

"I'm sure of that." He met her eyes again. "I meant what I said, though. I don't want to do anything like that again, and I think I'm old enough that I can make a decision that will last. I know some people, when they're young, they say I'll never do this or I'll never do that, and then when they get older, they do. But I know that with this, I won't. Even if I'm young, it's a long ways in my past, and it's going to stay there."

"I know. I believe you."

He was calmer now. He heard people talking in Spanish on the other side of the wagon, and he did not try to hear if they were talking about him. "Well, I need to go," he said. "I have to find my saddle and my other things."

She nodded, but neither of them moved.

His hands found hers.

"I hope nothing bad happens when I'm gone. I hope I'm able to come back and see you, but I can't say when."

"I hope so, too."

He still did not move. "I want to tell you something. It's about yesterday, when we were down by the water. Well, I felt something I never felt before. Actually, I mean, well, you're the only girl I ever kissed."

Her eyes were full and shining, but she did not say anything.

Now that he had started, he had to go on. "And I don't care if I ever meet another girl. Even if I can't see you again. I'll wait a long time."

"Don't worry," she said. "Everything passes."

He did not want to think about what Cushman might do to these people, but tears came to his eyes as he realized he might not ever see her again. He put his arms around her and lost himself in their kiss.

Milena's low voice brought them back to the present. *"Vamos, Anita."*

In a second she was gone. The voices in Spanish continued as he knelt beneath the wagon and dragged out his saddle, his bedroll, and his bag.

He did not speak to Lockwood as they saddled their horses next to one another, out on the grassy plain away from camp as the night drew in. Lockwood finished first and stood nearby, whistling a faint tune that sounded like "Green Grow the Lilacs." Tommy thought he was all too breezy, considering what had happened, but maybe he had had a sweet farewell with Milena.

When Tommy had his horse ready to go, Lockwood had quit whistling his tune. Lamplight showed from the camp, and the faint sound of voices carried.

"Let's walk 'em for a ways," said Lockwood. "Stretch our legs."

"You seem to be cheerful, considering what all went on."

"Like our friends say, *No hay remedio*. There's not much you can do about it."

"I realize things were stacked against us, but I thought you gave up pretty quick. Not to mention speaking for both of us."

"Ah, he's a hard one to argue with, that Faustino. He comes back every time with things twisted just a little bit different. And if you come right down to it, he's not far off on a couple of things."

"Which ones?"

"Well, for one, I think he's right about Cushman having it in for any white people who throw in with these people. I don't think it's Cushman's main reason, because, like I said yesterday, I think he's got a bigger kind of hate. I think Faustino's exaggerating, and I think he knows it. I argued with him about it yesterday and did all right, but today he had more cards, you might say."

"That's my fault."

"Oh, hell, don't worry about that. If it wasn't one thing, it would be another."

Tommy looked over his shoulder at the camp, which was getting smaller in the distance. Anita was there, growing more out of reach with every step. He looked ahead and kept walking. "Well, that's one. What's the other thing he's right about?"

Lockwood laughed. "Oh, the way he put it was funny, in his translated Spanish. But of course he was right. We do have an interest in the feminine persons, though he exaggerated that, too."

"Well, that gets to me as well. I can see where he's jealous of me. He has been from the start. But what does he care about you? He could have had her, and he turned her down. At least that's what Gabriel said."

Lockwood was silent, and only their footfalls and those of the horses sounded.

"Maybe I shouldn't have said that. I guess

you didn't know."

Lockwood's voice came back with spirit. "That's all right. It just took me a minute to put it together. He's a fool, I can say that. And furthermore, that's the way some men are. They don't want a woman, but they don't want anyone else to have her, either. That's just a problem he's got with his own underwear."

"Well, it helped him get rid of us, even if the clincher was about me."

"Huh. I'll tell you, there's another reason, as much as anything else, that made me think it might be just as well that we left for a while."

"What's that?"

"Ortiz. There's no good goin' to come of him at all."

"Faustino seems to think he's good protection."

"He might not get 'em all killed, but I don't see him as their salvation. If I ever saw a duck out of water, it's him. I don't think he'll last long around these people. They're too decent. Even Faustino, stiff-necked though he is."

"So you think we just wait him out? Ortiz, that is?"

"Better than being around him."

"I guess so. But I still don't like walking

out on those people."

"Ah, you know what they say. Absence makes the heart grow fonder."

Tommy almost laughed. "I can't imagine Faustino getting any fonder of us."

Lockwood's voice still had a light tone. "Oh, he might be glad to see us at some point. But I was referring to the others, you know. The feminine persons."

Chapter Thirteen

Tommy sat with his head held back as Lockwood fanned the campfire with his hat, bringing a brighter glow to the orange center. Thick smoke was rising in a lazy cloud. Lockwood shifted in his crouched position and made shorter, brisker motions with the hat. A small flame leapt up in the center of the twigs, spread, and grew higher. The flame burned cleaner, and the rising heat dispersed the heavy smoke.

"That's better," said Lockwood "I don't like all that thick smoke. You never know if someone else is around and wants to come and see what's going on." He settled onto his knees and reached for some thicker twigs to build up the fire.

Tommy shifted his eyes from the fire to the small can of water. Lockwood had shared a can of peaches from his meager store, and now he was going to boil some coffee in a can. The day was getting under way on a small scale and at a slow place. Tommy made an effort to be patient as Lockwood went about it all in his casual way.

"Ahh," said Lockwood. "Now she's burnin'. Sometimes I'm amazed at how much trouble you have to go to, and how much fire you need, just to boil a little coffee. It's a good thing we don't have to cook a pot of beans. 'Course, before the day's out, we might wish we had some beans."

"What kind of a plan have you got in mind for today?"

"Right now, the biggest thing for me is to get this to boil, and to try to keep it from spillin' over."

"And after that, I suppose the big thing is to drink the coffee."

"That would be next." Lockwood poked at the fire with a stick. "What's on your mind? You don't seem like you're in a very good mood."

"I don't see how I could be, after the way I was made to look yesterday. It was bad enough that they brought up that thing from the past, but then they laughed at me."

"Oh, that'll blow over. Might take a little time, but like you said, you put it in the past. Anybody who cares, if you know what I mean, ought to be able to see that. You did something unwise, but young people make mistakes, and everyone knows it. And furthermore, not to be unkind, you might have had a bit of bad company."

"I don't want to blame it on Red."

"Of course not. You stood up and admitted it, just like you should. Anyone who wants to be a man has got to own up for the things he did. And it helps if he learns from it."

"I think I have. I've thought about it, from the day we did it and even more so since it all came out in the open yesterday. I think I have a better sense of good and bad than I did when I was just a little younger — say, when I first came to work for Cushman."

Lockwood poked at the fire again. "Yeah, I know what you mean. All the time you're growin' up, they say, 'You know the difference between right and wrong, don't you?' And you say, 'sure.' But maybe what you really know is what will get you in trouble. That's not the same as knowin', deep down, why things are right or wrong to do."

"That's exactly what I mean."

Lockwood grimaced as he shaped up the burning pieces. "It's called a moral sense." He reached for three more sticks, about an inch thick, and laid them on top of the fire. "Not everyone gets it at the same point in

270

life. That's why some young people get in trouble. And, of course, some people don't get it ever, and that's why they end up in the bad ways they do."

"So if someone gets it, he can change."

"Sure, but he's got to stay with it. He doesn't just say, 'I'm sorry,' and go on to do something like it again. Not that I'm sayin' you would. I'm puttin' it in general terms."

"I understand." Tommy sorted things out for a few seconds. "So that's one kind of change. Now I've got a question about another kind."

"Go ahead. I seem to be the philosopher of the moment, but that's because there's only two of us here."

"Well, it goes back to the way I grew up. When my folks died, I lived with my aunt and uncle. They didn't have much, and I was used to that. But my uncle always said things like, 'A poor man has a poor way of doin' things,' and 'I was born poor, and I'll die poor.' So that's what I'm wondering, whether someone is stuck in a way of life where he started out or whether he can move up. I've always thought he could, or at least I hoped so, but when I get made fun of, I begin to wonder."

"If you mean whether a man can rise in the world, some people can. Some men, like

Lincoln and Grant, have risen quite a bit, but they're exceptional. And some of them, not to say which, have had a long ways to fall. In general, though, and this is just my idea, a man can make a better life for himself than he started out with, but he doesn't become an entirely different man."

"That's the way I meant it — whether a person who started out low can keep from being low for the rest of his life."

"I think so. It's a natural thing for people to want to do better in life, although not everybody tries, and not everyone who does try does it the same way. Some men want to cheat to get there." Lockwood laughed. "And there's the lowness comin' out. Then there's others who move up a level, or even two, and they try to pretend they're something they aren't. That is, they deny where they come from. And I think that comes out, too. Like I said, a fella doesn't change all that much. He starts out bein' Joe Jackson, and a little bit of money and some nice clothes aren't going to make him into Lord Chesterfield. But some men will try to make it seem like they're better than their own kind."

"I don't believe I've met anyone like that."

Lockwood smiled. "You're just gettin' started." He grimaced again as he faced the fire, which was blazing with the most recent sticks he had put on. "For the moment, though, it looks as if we might get some coffee."

"And after that?"

"Sooner or later, we'll have to get some more grub. But in the meanwhile, I'd like to look around in the neighborhood. I don't like the idea of leavin' our friends open to any more surprise attacks."

"I didn't like leaving to begin with."

"I know. But even if I was wrong, it seemed like the best idea at the time."

"Do you think Ortiz has finished his bottle of whiskey?"

"Oh, he's a bad pill. With or without a bottle."

Tommy followed Lockwood on horseback up out of the creek bottom and headed west. As long as they had been camped on the creek, Tommy felt connected to Anita. He imagined her a mile upstream, dipping a pail in the water. Now he was out in the open country, with no place to call home and no specific place where he was headed. Tommy's idea of the neighborhood, as Lockwood had called it, was bounded only by the creek on the east and the Mexican camp to the north.

Lockwood did not whistle or sing, and he did not make small talk. He rode in silence, stopping every once in a while to listen. On one occasion he dismounted and knelt to study the ground. A dry breeze had picked up from the southwest. Lockwood tore off a twist of shortgrass, tossed it into the air, and watched it float away. Without a word, he swung into the saddle again.

The sun was drawing close to straight-up noon when Lockwood stopped and pointed to the north. "I've been watching that dust for the last ten minutes," he said. "Headed east." He nudged his horse in that direction.

Tommy heaved a sigh. They had been wandering one way and another but mostly west, and now they were going back to where they started.

Lockwood drifted along for half a mile, then held up his hand and brought the grey horse to a stop. Tommy brought his horse alongside.

"I think there's more than one rider to make that much dust," said Lockwood. He held his hand out flat at the edge of his hat brim to extend the shade.

"It looks like they're going where we were camped."

"A little bit north, but I wouldn't be

surprised if they camp on that same creek."

"What do you want to do?"

"Get a look at 'em if we can."

Lockwood led the way, keeping higher ground to the left. Twice, at intervals of half a mile or so, he motioned for Tommy to wait as he rode up to the crest. Each time, he came back shaking his head.

A sparse tree line showed the course of the creek about a mile to the east. Lockwood had made another stop, and he sat with his hands on the saddle horn. He spoke in a low voice. "They ought to have gotten to the creek by now. If they cross it, I don't know what to think. Let me go take another look." He rode up the slope, stayed but a minute, and came back down. "I see smoke. I'd say they made camp."

"Do you think it's them?"

"I have a hunch it is, but I'm going to have to take a look." Lockwood brushed his mustache with his gloved hand. "It's not going to be easy. I'll have to go on foot. You wait with the horses, and you be ready to ride like hell if we have to."

Lockwood rode west again, following the contours until he found a low area that curved around to the north. After another ten minutes of roundabout riding, he came to a stop.

"Wait here," he said.

He rode uphill, made a half-circle with the horse, and rode back. He slid off the saddle and handed the reins to Tommy.

"This is as close as we're going to get with the horses," he said in a low voice. He unbuckled his saddlebag and took out a small pair of binoculars. "Keep an eye out."

He walked up the slope, carrying the binoculars away from him and leaning forward. At the top, he lowered into a crouch and disappeared over the brow.

Time dragged on as Tommy waited. Lockwood's horse moved, and Pete moved. The grey horse lowered its head to crop grass, and Tommy pulled up on the reins. The horse leaned its head forward and shook its saddle. No other sounds came from anywhere around.

The sun was straight up now and beating down. Tommy was sweating and could not feel the breeze in the low spot. The grey horse lifted its tail, and the smell of fresh manure drifted on the warm air. Pete shifted his weight.

The grey horse's head rose up, and the animal snuffled.

"Shhh!" said Tommy.

Here came Bill Lockwood, carrying his binoculars and digging in his heels as he hustled down the slope.

"Did anyone see you?"

"Nah. But it's them, all right." Lockwood put his binoculars away and took the reins from Tommy. "There's five of 'em."

Tommy made a quick tally. Vince Cushman, Lew Greer, Walt McKinney, Fred Berwick, and one bulldog. "That sounds right," he said.

"It sure doesn't look like they're out workin' cattle. They've got one horse each and hardly any camp gear. No wagon and supplies, for sure." Lockwood pushed back his hat. "They don't look like they're up to any good."

"What do you think we should do?"

Lockwood dragged his cuff across his forehead. "I think we should go warn our friends."

No one stopped them as they rode up to the Mexican camp and dismounted. A gathering had formed inside. Lockwood left Tommy with the horses and walked straight to Raimundo. Tommy looked around for Anita but did not see her. He refocused on the center of the camp.

Faustino and Ortiz stood about three yards apart, neither of them speaking. A strange tension filled the air. Faustino was not wearing a hat, and his full head of dark hair was shining in the sun. He stood with his hands on his hips, above the handles of his two revolvers. Ortiz was wearing his black leather vest and his flat-crowned hat as before, but his posture sagged, and his face had a sour expression.

Gabriel appeared at Tommy's left.

"What's going on?" Tommy asked.

"Nothing but trouble. This man Alfredo is very drunk."

"He looks like it. How much whiskey did he have?"

"He drank the whole bottle last night. Then he tried to touch Milena. Everyone knows he's dangerous, so they keep an eye on him until he goes to sleep. Then this morning, when the women all go out to make a circle, he looks in my uncle's wagon for another bottle. He finds one and drinks it all."

Tommy felt a sense of embarrassment and dread together. The women had their routine of forming a circle, all of them looking outward, as they took turns at a latrine they scratched in the middle. All along, Tommy had done as the other men did, pretending not to notice. Now Ortiz, drunken and callous, had disrespected that sense of privacy at the same time he had trespassed into someone else's quarters and had stolen something.

Tommy glanced at Ortiz's holster. The gun was not there.

Faustino spoke in Spanish, and Tommy was able to follow the meaning. *You get on your horse, and you go. Do not come back. Not here, and not in our pueblo.*

Movement caught Tommy's eye. Emilio came around from the north side of the wagons, leading the horse Ortiz had ridden the day before. It was saddled with a bedroll tied on back.

Faustino looked over his shoulder and nodded at his brother. Facing Ortiz again and motioning with his thumb, he said, *"Vamos."*

Ortiz stood in place, swaying in his drunkenness. His face held the same sagging, unpleasant expression as he moistened his lips and made a spitting motion at the ground in front of him. He said something that Tommy did not understand, but it must have fallen short of vulgarity, for it caused Faustino to fold his arms across his chest and breathe out through his nose rather than step forward and punch the drunk man.

Ortiz walked toward the saddled horse

and stopped a yard away. *"Mi pistola,"* he said.

Emilio produced the gun, drawing it from his waistband in back. He held it barrel up and clicked the cylinder to show that the gun was not loaded. He stuck it in Ortiz's holster, then reached into his pocket, brought out a handful of cartridges, and put them in the pocket of Ortiz's vest.

Emilio held the horse's reins as Ortiz grabbed the saddle horn with both hands. The man staggered as he tried to put his boot in the stirrup, so Emilio moved forward and boosted Ortiz with his shoulder. Ortiz found his seat, took his reins, and turned the horse around. Slow and solitary, with his hat tipped against the breeze on his right, he rode to the southeast as half the people in the camp watched him.

A hundred yards out, he took his gun from the holster and began loading it. He flinched once and reached down, to no avail, but to all appearances he got the rest of the shells into the cylinder. Still slouched, he kept riding, with low dust rising and blowing away in the breeze. He crossed the creek and continued heading southeast, in the direction he had come from with the Romero brothers the day before.

The people in camp drifted back to their

wagons, some inside the enclosure and some outside. Faustino and Emilio had taken seats on wooden boxes, as if it were not worth their attention to watch Ortiz ride away. Faustino had his usual self-confident air, which Tommy attributed to his successful exercise in authority — in spite of his having brought the man into camp to begin with. As for himself, Tommy did not feel as if all of his blame was gone, but he didn't mind seeing Ortiz, his main accuser, leaving in disgrace.

Raimundo stood up to face Faustino as Lockwood moved to a position closer to the opening where Tommy stood with the horses.

Raimundo spoke in English. "Well, Faustino, it's a good thing you got rid of that man. I don't know how much good he would have done us. I always thought he was a criminal, and there's the proof."

"Well, he's gone, and that's that. No need to say I told you so." Faustino wrinkled his nose. "And what brings your friends back so soon?"

"They come to tell us that Cooshmon has a camp not far away. Five of them. Bill doesn't think that the one you shot is with them."

Faustino flicked a glance at Lockwood.

"He wasn't here. How would he know which one it is?"

"By counting. And you may remember, Tommy was here."

Faustino shrugged.

Lockwood spoke up. "They don't look like they've got any kind of a cow camp. I think they're here for trouble."

"Then it's a good thing you aren't out there alone. They might hurt you."

"I wouldn't laugh. You know what they're capable of." Lockwood held his hands at his sides. "For what it's worth, I'm offering to help once again. Yesterday you said you had enough help, but your man left just as easy as he came. Well, maybe not quite as easy. And I'll give you credit for gettin' rid of him the way you did."

"No one got hurt. It would have been very bad for him if someone did."

Lockwood turned to Raimundo. "If you don't mind, I've got a suggestion."

"Go ahead. I'll listen."

"I don't know what Cushman is up to, but I think he'll make a move of one kind or another. He's got his camp south of here. If he does anything, he'll start from there. So I think you should move all the sheep north of camp, and put all the horses and donkeys on the north side of the wagons, between the camp and the sheep. Make sure we've got water in camp, and don't let anybody get very far away."

Raimundo glanced at Gabriel. "I think Bill has a good idea. Go tell the others to move the sheep. You help them."

Lockwood said, "Tommy, I'll take care of the horses. You can get started hauling water. Make sure all the buckets are full."

Gabriel left to go to the sheep. Lockwood took the reins of the two horses and led them away. Raimundo said something to Faustino ending with the word *caballos* and followed Lockwood. Faustino and Emilio stood up and headed for their two wagons.

The camp had emptied out pretty fast. Tommy glanced around at the wooden boxes, one vacant chair, a small pile of folded canvas, and an empty washtub. He walked to the other end of the camp, looking for buckets. At the tailgate of the Villarreals' wagon, he came face-to-face with Anita.

She was wearing a red-and-brown dress with a low collar. Her long, dark hair fell loose below her shoulders and waved in the breeze at the edge of camp. A wave of emotion overtook him, a mixture of wonder and yearning. He stood with his eyes wide open, not knowing what to say.

"You came back," she said. "See? I told you."

He took her hands and gazed into her soft, dark eyes. "I didn't know when I would see you again." His eyes roved over her clear, tan face and open neck. Maybe it was the way he felt, but she did not look like a girl to him. She looked like a young woman. He pressed her hands in his, and she returned the pressure. "We came back for a serious reason," he said. "Bill saw Cushman and his men in a camp about a mile from here."

"Do you think they will come today?"

"No telling. They just got there and set their camp, started their fire. So you'd think they're not going to move for a while. The first two times they attacked, they did it at night. But you never know. So the men are moving all the animals. Bill told me to bring in a supply of water." Still holding her hands, he lost himself for a second in her eyes. Then he pulled himself back. "Where are those two buckets that make you look so pretty when you carry them?"

She smiled as she withdrew her hands. "I'll get them."

In less than a minute she returned.

"Thanks," he said, reaching for the handles.

"Let me help."

"I think it would be better if you stayed here. Bill said for me to fill all the buckets, so if you can get some more together, I'll go fill these." He held his hands out, and she handed the buckets forward. But she did not release them until he kissed her. "I'll be right back," he said.

He left camp on a fast walk, happy that Bill had given him the job he did. When he reached the creek, his sense of caution set in again. He kept an eye about him as he dipped the two buckets in the water.

On his way up the hill, he saw the sheep moving. The herders were pushing them toward the west side of camp. The animals raised wisps of dust and particles of dry grass, and the breeze carried the distinct odor of sheep.

Inside the enclosure, Tommy set the two buckets on the ground and took the two empties that Anita handed him. He pursed his lips at her and set off for the next trip.

The sun had moved into early afternoon by the time he had eleven buckets and two washtubs full of water. The other men and boys had moved all the animals. Faustino and Emilio sat on boxes on their side of the enclosure, while Raimundo and Lockwood sat on their side. Tommy and Gabriel sat on the ground. It was the same seating arrangement as the evening before, with the exception that Ortiz was gone and someone had taken the chair away. Tommy imagined Ortiz still riding at his slow pace, perhaps stewing about how things had turned out, perhaps taking in the sagebrush and grass and prickly pear through dull eyes as the effect of the liquor wore off. At least he was out of the way.

From where he sat, Tommy could see two chickens picking at the ground outside the wagon at the far end of camp. To the right of that wagon, a group of children laughed as they played with a dog. One of the women he had never spoken to was hanging children's clothing on a rope stretched between two wagons. Beyond her, Tommy saw the swishing tail of a brown horse and the lowered head of the sand-colored burro with the striped cross on his front quarters.

Milena and Eusebia appeared with plates of food and handed them out in the same arrangement as the evening before. No one made a comment except for the usual courtesies of thank you and you're welcome. When Tommy received his plate, it consisted of a serving of cold beans with a few pieces of cold meat on the side. For his part, it was an improvement over breakfast, so he dug in.

The meal did not last long. Everyone ate in a businesslike manner, and no offers came for second helpings. One by one, the plates went away.

Faustino took out his pocketknife and was rubbing his thumb across the edge of the blade when he stopped and frowned. He wrinkled his nose and looked up. *"Huele a humo,"* he said.

Tommy looked at Gabriel.

"He says it smells like smoke."

Lockwood stood up. "No one has had a fire going, have they?"

Raimundo looked up from his seat and shook his head.

Within a few seconds, Tommy and Gabriel had joined the four men at the opening of the camp. They were all turned toward the southwest, facing into the breeze. Women and children had gathered at the other end of the camp, gazing in the same direction.

Smoke was lifting off the ground in a line about two hundred yards across. Low flames licked into the grey cloud, which rose and thinned out in the wind.

"It sure is a fire," said Lockwood. "We've got to try to stop it." He looked around at the others. "We'll have to go out in the open, but we don't have much of a choice."

CHAPTER FOURTEEN

A frenzy took over the camp as several people shouted orders at once. Faustino and Raimundo had an argument about whether the group should try to hitch up and pull out or whether the people should stay and fight off the fire. Raimundo prevailed, saying that Cushman's men could shoot their horses and burros and leave the whole group in a worse position. Meanwhile, Lockwood was calling for gunnysacks, while women were ordering children to take cover. Two dogs were barking, children were crying, and one goat that was tied to a wagon was bleating.

Anita came out of the confusion and asked Tommy, "What does he want? What does Bill want?"

"Gunnysacks." Seeing that she didn't understand, Tommy said, "Burlap bags. You know, like grain sacks."

Her face lit up. "Oh, yes. Come with me."

She led the way to her aunt's wagon, where Eusebia and Leonila sat holding each other in the lee and shadow of the wagon box. Anita spoke quickly and climbed up into the wagon. She dug through blankets and valises, then leaned over and pulled up a bundle of burlap bags.

"Perfect," said Tommy. "Just the thing."

She tossed it to him, and he caught it. He did not wait for her but took off on a run. He found Lockwood trying to make himself understood to Milena. He was making a rectangular figure with his hands and saying, *"Bolsa. Bolsa."* When he saw the bundle, he pointed and said, *"Sí, sí. Bolsa."*

"Costal," said Milena. *"Costal de yute."*

Tommy flopped the bundle on the ground, and Lockwood dug out his pocketknife. He cut the twine that bound the sacks, then pulled out two loose bags. He gave one to Milena and took one himself to a nearby tub. He plunged the bag into the water and sloshed it up and down. Milena did the same in the next tub.

"Jesus," said Lockwood. "Three words for everything, and I know two. *Bolsa. Saco.* Come to find out they call it a *costal.*" He looked at Milena and said, "What the hell is *yute*?"

She understood that much English. She

paused in her soaking and held up a corner of the burlap. She rubbed her thumb on the coarse woven fabric. *"Yute,"* she said, in two clear syllables.

"Gracias," said Lockwood. Then to Tommy, "There's three words for fire, too, but it's in plain view, so all you have to do is point. Damn, these things take forever to soak up the water. Okay. We'll go with these two. You keep soaking more of these." He pulled the dripping burlap bag out of the tub, and a stream of water ran off of it. "Here," he said, calling to Raimundo and then handing it to him. He pulled the other sack out of Milena's tub, again spilling water. *"Más,"* he said, and he took off on a run, bending over with the weight of the soaked burlap.

Milena was poking the next bag with a stick to move it up and down in the tub. Tommy sloshed the bag he was working on. The level of the water had gone down in the tub with just one bag, and he could see they were going to need more water before this was through.

Faustino and Emilio took the next two heavy, dripping bags and ran for the front line. Milena and Gabriel began soaking the next pair of sacks as Tommy poured two buckets of water into each tub. He hurried over to the opening and looked out.

The four men were beating at the flames with the burlap sacks. Sparks and black debris flew up. The men coughed and kept swatting as the smoke billowed up and over them. Tommy did not see any of Cushman's men. He imagined they were waiting to see how things developed. The sound of voices at the water tubs reminded him that he needed to go back.

Two men had come in from the sheep and were waiting for the next two sacks. Tommy figured it was a good time to fetch more water, so he grabbed two buckets and ran down the hill. He yanked the buckets open-mouthed against the current, thinking he would fill them faster that way, but he was wrong. He had to settle down and fill each bucket with a steady hold. When they were both full, he ran with them back to the camp.

Gabriel and Milena were sloshing away at the next two bags. Four buckets were empty. Tommy set down the two full ones, picked up two empties, and took off. Halfway down the slope, he looked back. Anita was following.

"Go back!" he hollered.

"I'm going to help."

"Go back. You'll get hurt."

She set the buckets down and ran back.

Tommy went on his way. He was filling the first bucket with his deliberate method when Anita surprised him by showing up. She carried two empty buckets in one hand and the chokecherry club in the other.

"We need to hurry," he said. He set the full bucket on a level spot and bent to fill the next one.

A familiar voice sounded in back of him. "Just hold it right there, kid."

Both Tommy and Anita jerked around to see lean-jawed Walt McKinney holding a gun. His small upper teeth were closed down on his lower lip, and he had a few days of stubble on his face. As usual, his clothes were wrinkled and in need of a wash.

"Now take your gun out real slow, kid, and hand it to me, butt first."

"What do you think you're doing?"

"What I'm told. Now you do the same, or you'll end up with a hole in you."

"You're a real traitor, aren't you?"

"Don't make me cry. Now give me the gun." McKinney's eyes flickered. "Get out of the way, little sister."

Anita kept the club behind her as she moved aside.

McKinney stepped forward, took Tommy's gun, and stuck it in his own holster. Stepping back, he waved his yellow-handled Colt at Tommy and then at Anita. "Now give me the stick, girl. It's too big for you anyway." He lunged in an apparent attempt to catch her by surprise, but she swung with the empty buckets. He grabbed a handle and yanked, pulling her forward. The club slipped from her grasp and swung away. McKinney yanked again, and Anita let go of the bucket he had a hold of. The movement threw him off balance for a second, long enough for Tommy to pick up the club. McKinney flung the bucket aside, got his footing, and brought his pistol up to get it pointed at Tommy.

He wasn't quite fast enough. Tommy brought the club up and around and fetched McKinney a good one behind his left ear. McKinney's narrow-brimmed hat tumbled away, and his yellow-handled pistol fell in the dirt. McKinney himself dropped like a sack of potatoes and went still.

Tommy stood back with the club in his hand, waiting to see if McKinney would move. When he didn't, Tommy said, "There's no time to feel sorry. We still need to fill these buckets and get back before someone else comes." He stood over Mc-Kinney, rolled the body a quarter of a turn, and pulled his six-gun from the holster.

Standing up, he looked around and located the yellow-handled Colt. He picked it up, holstered his own gun, and stuck the Colt in his belt.

He made short work of filling the rest of the buckets. He positioned them so he could grab and carry two with each hand. "Let me do this," he said to Anita. "It's not far. You can carry the stick."

Back in camp, Milena and Gabriel had reached a lull, as each of them had a bag soaking in the tub. Tommy set down the full buckets and took careful steps to the edge of camp. He expected to see more of Cushman's men, but all he saw was the line of six men from camp, all of them beating at the burning ground, scattering sparks and ashes and black particles.

Tommy ran back to the tubs. "Let's take two more," he said. He pulled at the sodden bag in Milena's tub. He could not believe how heavy it was. As he hauled it out of the tub, the water level went down, and runnels flowed off the folds in the burlap.

Just as he was about to pull the soaking mass toward him, he recalled the gun in his belt. He dropped the sack in the water, pulled out the gun, and looked around. Gabriel was on his way to the fire line. Tommy handed the pistol to Milena, and she put it in her apron pocket. He bent over and lifted the burden again from the water. He tried to fold the sack, but it was too ungainly, so he bunched it and hugged it as he took off running.

Lockwood hollered at him and waved for him to come over. When he got there, Lockwood was standing up but not straight, and he was taking deep breaths. "Give me that one," he said. "I've just about beat all the water out of mine. You can take it back."

"I came to help."

"You can help by taking this back to camp and staying there."

"But you're all done in."

Lockwood gave him a hard look. The man's face was streaked with sweat and dark ash, and his easygoing air was gone. "Don't make me mad, kid. There's women and children back there, and if any of these sons of bitches get in, there'd better be someone to help. And don't be afraid to shoot, for Christ's sake."

"I'm not."

"Good. Now get back there."

Tommy took the tattered bag, grimy and almost dry, and headed back to camp. Halfway there, he thought to look back, and he saw Gabriel carrying a worn bag as well. From the way he cradled it with one end flopping against his shoulder, he made Tommy think of a woman fleeing a burning city and carrying a baby.

Inside the camp, the next two bags were ready to go. Tommy picked up the first one and tried rolling it. The bag was still bulky and awkward, but it was manageable. Tommy just finished rolling it when Gabriel showed up and said, "I'll take it."

Tommy handed it to him and began rolling the next one. The whole process was a sloppy business, with water spilling on the ground, making mud as well as soaking Tommy's shirt and pants. But it had to be done, so Tommy hung with it. He wrapped his arms around the dripping bundle and took off again for the fire line. Up ahead, Gabriel was making the exchange with Faustino, so Tommy headed toward Emilio. He stopped long enough to trade the soggy bag for the frayed, half-dry bag, then turned and broke into a run again.

As he did, he lost hold of one corner of the burlap, the front half of the bag fell down lengthwise, and he stepped on the free end. Down he went, losing his hat and plowing his face in the dirt. He scrambled to his feet and gathered up the bag, then fetched his hat. Looking around, he saw all six men beating at the burning prairie. Up ahead, Gabriel was running into the enclosure. Tommy was glad no one had seen him, to make him feel like a fool; then he realized that everyone had to look out for himself. If he had twisted an ankle or broken his leg, no one would have seen that, either.

Off and running, Tommy had almost reached the wagons, and was thinking about nothing more complicated than a wet burlap bag, when he heard a shot. He surged forward and dashed into the enclosure. He tossed the bag toward the tub Milena was tending with her stick. Gabriel was bent over the other tub, pushing down on a bag and sending up bubbles. Anita was pouring water into her brother's tub. Tommy ran back to the edge of the camp.

Down the slope in the haze of smoke and dust and particles, two riders were charging at the men who were fighting the fire. The horsemen had come in behind the men on foot and were riding back and forth on the unburned grass. Both riders were large, hulking figures. Through the haze, Tommy recognized Lew Greer on a large roan he often used. The other man rode a sorrel horse that Red used to ride, so Tommy assumed that he was the second bulldog.

As the men rode back and forth, charging and wheeling, they created a melee.

Raimundo and the two men who had come from the sheep herd did not have weapons, so they faced the riders and darted to one side and another. Emilio was lying on the ground, pressing his hand to his thigh. Lockwood had his gun drawn, and he was moving from one side to another, trying to pick up a target. Faustino had both guns drawn and was standing square. He raised his right arm and fired just as the bulldog shot at him. The reports made a *pop-pop!* succession, and the heavy rider slumped and grabbed his saddle horn.

Greer was wheeling. He came around with his gun drawn, then spurred his horse to make it bolt. He rode past his companion and showed no intention of helping. Instead, he aimed across the saddle and fired at Faustino, who fired back and kicked up dirt halfway to the wagons. Greer kept going on the large roan, which was picking up speed with its head stretched out. Greer fired one, two, three, but he was going too fast to hit anything except by accident. Faustino, with his feet still planted, shot four times, twice with each pistol, but he couldn't catch up with his target.

Lockwood, meanwhile, was turning, and his arm was sweeping. His gun barked, and Greer lurched in the saddle. He dropped his pistol and grabbed the saddle horn with both hands. He lost his reins, so the roan horse held his head to one side with the reins trailing in the air. Greer bobbled in his seat but held on as the horse galloped west. The other rider loped after him, the two of them looking like large hunchbacks on their way to torture a village. Half a mile out, the second rider tumbled from the saddle and lay still on the prairie. Greer kept on riding.

Faustino hollered and gestured to the others to keep fighting the fire, and then he ran to tend to his brother. The other men resumed the heavy work of slapping the burning grass.

Tommy decided he would carry down a wet bag of his own and join the fight. He turned around and was pushing off to run to the water tubs when he stopped short, blocked by the large form of Vinch Cushman.

Like a huge raven from the world of dreams, Cushman towered over him, a broad, dusky figure with his back to the sun, looming in his dustcoat and floppy-brimmed hat. His dark pistol pointed at Tommy, and though his face lay in shadow, his beak-like nose and yellowed eyes were prominent and terrible. Spit flew as his deep voice pierced the air. "Stop right there, you pissant!"

Tommy stopped, almost paralyzed. Fear had jolted him in the stomach, and his mouth had gone dry as cotton. Beyond Cushman, he saw Fred Berwick holding Milena, Gabriel, and Anita at gunpoint. *The ultimate traitor,* Tommy thought. *The Judas goat.*

Cushman's voice rumbled out of his cavernous chest. "Give me your gun."

Tommy was so dazed that he felt detached from himself.

Cushman moved a step closer and shoved his pistol into Tommy's cheekbone. "I said give me your gun, or I'll pull this trigger."

Tommy's hand was shaking as he handed over his six-gun.

"Good. Now get over here with your friends." Cushman put the gun in the pocket of his coat.

When Tommy reached the group, Fred Berwick gave him a dead-wall expression and stepped back. Cushman shoved Tommy so that he ended up in the midst of the other three.

The deep voice grated on Tommy and made him shiver. "This is better than I thought. Got four all at once, like rats in a cage. And two of 'em are breeders." Sunlight fell on Cushman's face as his head hung forward, and his eyes, one larger than the other, looked over his prize. The corners of his mouth went down, and his nostrils flared. Then the vile expression subsided. He said, "Here's how we'll do it, Fred. We'll put these four away, and then we'll pick off the others as they come up the hill." He pointed his pistol at Tommy. "Start with this one first."

Tommy backed up a short step and was jostled by Anita. He could feel Milena's hands pressing him, giving him support. Gabriel was on his left. Fred Berwick was standing four feet away and would not look at any of them. His spectacles glinted in the sunlight, and his blue eyes looked sick with worry.

"You said not to shoot unless they shot first," he said. "Don't fire until fired upon. We can't just shoot these four."

Cushman's voice blared. "What the hell? They've already shot at us today. For all I know, they got Arlen or Lew. This is no time to pussyfoot."

Fred's mouth was screwed up, and his chin was working back and forth. "This isn't the way we're supposed to do it."

"Don't tell me how to do it. We get it done. I told you to shoot this little maggot. Don't waste time thinking about it."

Fred shook his head. "I can't. I can't."

Cushman pointed his pistol at Fred. "Don't cross me now, you son of a bitch. Do what I say."

Tommy was frozen, and time seemed to draw out. His heart was racing as he expected something to happen. Then he felt Milena nudging him with a solid object. He put his hand in back of him, and the metal cylinder of a pistol touched his fingers. He kept his eyes glued on Cushman. He wondered why Cushman was forcing Fred into firing the first shot — whether he wanted Fred to share the guilt, or whether he, Cushman, had some hesitation himself. Tommy thought it was the latter. As soon as Fred took part, Cushman would blaze away.

Fred's eyes had a lost expression, and his voice quavered. "I can't. Not like this."

"Well, you're as bad as the rest." Cushman's six-gun blasted, tearing a ragged red spot in Fred's clean tan shirt. His hat fell forward onto his spectacles as his head snapped backward. He still held his pistol as he stumbled and his feet went out from under him.

Cushman held him in a hard gaze for a couple of seconds, long enough for Tommy to get his hand into position on Walt McKinney's revolver. He brought the gun around and cocked it, found the biggest part of the middle of Vinch Cushman, and shattered the afternoon as he pulled the trigger.

Cushman's arms went up like wings, and he seemed to rise in his boots, his eyes wide in surprise and rage. He leaned back, almost floating, and he fell as if he had stepped backward over a cliff. After he hit the ground, his cape-like coat settled like a layer of feathers, and his body went still. A seam of blood formed on his lips and at the corners of his mouth.

Tommy held the gun forward with both hands. His body was shaking, but he exerted control out through his arms and held the gun steady. After a long moment, he lowered the weapon.

Anita and Gabriel stood wide-eyed and silent.

Milena said, *"Está muerto."*

Tommy knew those words. *He's dead.* Tommy nodded his head, taking in the magnitude of what he had done. Clubbing Walt McKinney had been almost a reflex, but this had been a deliberate, focused action that he could reconstruct in steps. It had all happened in an instant, but it had its separate parts with no turning back. He had risen to action, and it was done. *"Sí,"* he said. *"Está muerto."*

CHAPTER FIFTEEN

The caravan had just pulled out of camp and was heading west when Bill Lockwood came riding back. He had left ahead of the group in order to carry the news to Fenton that someone should ride out to verify the scene and take care of the bodies. Now he had returned already.

He rode up to Raimundo's wagon where Tommy poked along on his good horse, Pete. "I found Lew Greer," he said. "About a mile west and a little ways south. So there's five to report. Just thought I'd let you know."

Raimundo said, "Thanks, Bill. We'll see you later."

Lockwood and Tommy stood on the downstream side of the earthen dam, while Raimundo and Faustino stood on the upstream side. Each one had a shovel, and they were cutting a channel to meet in the middle of the mound of dirt. None of the men seemed to be in a hurry, but no one lagged. They all dug at a steady pace. The sooner they cut into the reservoir, the sooner the creek would regain its flow.

Tommy wondered if he was the only one to feel excitement. Even the presence of the water seemed filled with energy. And getting to this moment had taken a great deal of resistance and fighting back on the part of the whole group. For his own part, he was surprised he had risen to the challenge, and yet he had done what had seemed like the only way out. It had made a difference. He was no longer a boy in the eyes of these men. He was one of them. They had chosen him to be part of the small crew for what amounted to a ceremony.

Behind the men, on the slope above the dry creek bed, the rest of the villagers waited. Men, women, children, goats, burros, and horses seemed to hold their collective breath as only a light murmur floated on the air. Tommy could feel Anita's attention. He knew that she, like the others, was waiting to see the water flow, and he felt a great pride in knowing that she saw him working with her father and the other men.

The two trenches were getting closer, and there was not enough room for four shovels.

Lockwood stood back, as did Faustino. Raimundo stood poised with his shovel as he left the last barrier of dirt for Tommy to scoop away. Tommy made his cut and lifted out a shovel full of dirt.

"Ahí va," said Raimundo. There it goes.

The first rush of water came rolling an inch deep across the dry dirt in the trench. The water was muddy, and foam gathered on the surface. The water rose and fell across the tiny ridges in the bottom. At last the murky tide flowed all the way through the channel and spread out to sink into the dry creek bed. Raimundo scraped the length of the trench with the point of his shovel, and the flow increased. He scraped again and again, dragging mud out to the lower end, until the water ran three inches deep and the width of a shovel head. Now the water was flowing in the creek.

Raimundo stood back and raised his shovel in victory. Tommy did the same, as did Lockwood and then Faustino. The crowd cheered and whistled and hollered. Tommy felt his eyes moisten as he saw Anita smiling and clapping.

"That's good," said Lockwood in his usual calm manner. "Let 'er flow. It'll take a while to clear the mud out, but there's enough water backed up to push it through. When it gets down to its normal level, it'll run clear."

Faustino said nothing. All this time he had been working as if in a silent truce, and even raising his shovel had seemed to be a reluctant concession.

Raimundo nodded in agreement, then looked across the ditch, smiling. "What do you say, Tommy?"

Tommy's foremost thought was about how happy he was to have Anita watching him, but he appreciated having a say. Gathering his repose, he leaned on his shovel and watched the water flow. He said, "I think it's moving all right. By this time tomorrow, we should have good water."

ABOUT THE AUTHOR

John D. Nesbitt lives in the plains country of Wyoming, where he teaches English and Spanish at Eastern Wyoming College. He writes western, contemporary, mystery, and retro/noir fiction as well as nonfiction and poetry. John has won many awards for his work, including two awards from the Wyoming State Historical Society (for fiction), two awards from Wyoming Writers for encouragement of other writers and service to the organization, two Wyoming Arts Council literary fellowships (one for fiction, one for nonfiction), two Will Rogers Medallion Awards, and three Spur awards from Western Writers of America. His most recent books are *Dark Prairie* and *Justice at Redwillow,* frontier mysteries with Five Star.

The employees of Thorndike Press hope you have enjoyed this Large Print book. All our Thorndike, Wheeler, and Kennebec Large Print titles are designed for easy reading, and all our books are made to last. Other Thorndike Press Large Print books are available at your library, through selected bookstores, or directly from us.

For information about titles, please call:
  (800) 223-1244

or visit our Web site at:
  http://gale.cengage.com/thorndike

To share your comments, please write:
  Publisher
  Thorndike Press
  10 Water St., Suite 310
  Waterville, ME 04901